AROUND CHI-TOWN

May: It's wedding bells once again for the Connellys. This time, they're ringing for the newest member of Chicago's "royal family"—Dr. Doug Connelly. In a private ceremony downtown, he wed nurse Maura Chambers. Kudos to her for landing Chicago's best-looking pediatrician since George Clooney's Dr. Ross.

It was just a short while ago that patriarch Grant Connelly was reunited with his long-lost illegitimate sons, twins Doug and Chance Barnett. The latter, a Navy SEAL, is reported to be off on yet another secret mission.

Not even the presence of two more powerful Connelly men could prevent a near-disaster at Connelly Corporation last night when a computer crash nearly wiped out the giant's software. A company spokesman said they're not ruling out sabotage.

With his meteoric rise to the top of the American business scene and his beautiful, former-princess wife, Grant must surely be the target of the green-eyed monster. But exactly who has it in for the well-respected Chicago icon?

Dear Reader,

Looking for romances with a healthy dose of passion? Don't miss Silhouette Desire's red-hot May lineup of passionate, powerful and provocative love stories!

Start with our MAN OF THE MONTH, *His Majesty, M.D.*, by bestselling author Leanne Banks. This latest title in the ROYAL DUMONTS miniseries features an explosive engagement of convenience between a reluctant royal and a determined heiress. Then, in Kate Little's *Plain Jane & Doctor Dad,* the new installment of Desire's continuity series DYNASTIES: THE CONNELLYS, a rugged Connelly sweeps a pregnant heroine off her feet.

A brooding cowboy learns about love and family in *Taming Blackhawk,* a SECRETS! title by Barbara McCauley. Reader favorite Sara Orwig offers a brand-new title in the exciting TEXAS CATTLEMAN'S CLUB: THE LAST BACHELOR series. In *The Playboy Meets His Match,* enemies become lovers and then some.

A sexy single mom is partnered with a lonesome rancher in Kathie DeNosky's *Cassie's Cowboy Daddy*. And in Anne Marie Winston's *Billionaire Bachelors: Garrett,* sparks fly when a tycoon shares a cabin with the woman he believes was his stepfather's mistress.

Bring passion into your life this month by indulging in all six of these sensual sizzlers.

Enjoy!

Joan Marlow Golan

Joan Marlow Golan
Senior Editor, Silhouette Desire

Please address questions and book requests to:
Silhouette Reader Service
U.S.: 3010 Walden Ave., P.O. Box 1325, Buffalo, NY 14269
Canadian: P.O. Box 609, Fort Erie, Ont. L2A 5X3

Plain Jane & Doctor Dad

KATE LITTLE

Silhouette
Desire

Published by Silhouette Books
America's Publisher of Contemporary Romance

Special thanks and acknowledgment are given
to Kate Little for her contribution to
the DYNASTIES: THE CONNELLYS series.

SILHOUETTE BOOKS

ISBN 0-373-76436-7

PLAIN JANE & DOCTOR DAD

Copyright © 2002 by Harlequin Books S.A.

This edition published by arrangement with Harlequin Books S.A.

® and TM are trademarks of Harlequin Books S.A., used under license. Trademarks indicated with ® are registered in the United States Patent and Trademark Office, the Canadian Trade Marks Office and in other countries.

Visit Silhouette at www.eHarlequin.com

Printed in U.S.A.

Books by Kate Little

Silhouette Desire

Jingle Bell Baby #1043
Husband for Keeps #1276
The Determined Groom #1302
The Millionaire Takes a Bride #1349
The Bachelorette #1401
Tall, Dark & Cranky #1422
Plain Jane & Doctor Dad #1436

KATE LITTLE

claims to have lots of experience with romance—"the *fictional* kind, that is," she is quick to clarify. She has been both an author and an editor of romance fiction for over fifteen years. She believes that a good romance will make the reader experience all the tension, thrills and agony of falling madly, deeply and wildly in love. She enjoys watching the characters in her books go crazy for each other, but hates to see the blissful couple disappear when it's time for them to live happily ever after. In addition to writing romance novels, Kate also writes fiction and nonfiction for young adults. She lives on Long Island, New York, with her husband and daughter.

DYNASTIES:
THE
CONNELLYS

MEET THE CONNELLYS

Meet the Connellys of Chicago—
wealthy, powerful and rocked by scandal,
betrayal...and passion!

Who's Who in *PLAIN JANE & DOCTOR DAD*

Dr. Doug Connelly—Within months, he found his
long-lost father, Grant Connelly, and a family-to-be
with pregnant Maura. But can the divorced doctor let
them into his barricaded heart?

Maura Chambers—Though pregnant and alone, she
vowed to give her baby everything—everything but
a father. Then Doug offered his name.... Dare Maura
hope for more?

Angie Donahue—Years ago she loved Grant Connelly
and gave him a child.... Now she's back—not for a
reunion, but for revenge.

One

As Nurse Maura Chambers left Scott's office, she knew she'd never see him again. But he didn't say "Good luck" or even "Good-bye." He merely shuffled papers around on his desk as she slipped through the doorway, ignoring her, as if she had already vanished from his sight.

She stepped from the quiet chamber into the busy hospital corridor, resisting the urge to give his door one last, resounding slam. What good would that do her now? It would only give the major-league gossips on staff more to talk about. Hadn't they already gotten enough mileage out of her failed romance? Anyway, in a matter of days Scott would be gone for good, starting a new job and a new life hundreds of miles away. And she'd be free of him. Almost.

Maura took a deep breath and started down the

crowded hallway, willing herself to look as busy as everyone around her. She kept her gaze downcast, avoiding eye contact with anyone who might stop her to ask why she looked so upset. She didn't feel like talking about her problems now. Not to anyone.

As much as she'd dreaded facing Scott Walker again, she'd been obligated to disclose her secret. After all, he bore his fair share of responsibility. But it only took a moment for Maura to realize Scott didn't see the matter that way. Not at all. His reaction had been more than disappointing. More than cold or unsympathetic. His attitude and succinct advice had made her sick to her stomach.

Well, what did you *really* expect? she asked herself. Haven't you known for weeks now what kind of man he is? It had been clear to her ever since the night Scott had announced, out of the blue, that he was leaving Chicago General. Leaving the city entirely for a new job as a hospital administrator in Minneapolis. Why would he be any different now?

Looking back, she felt angry all over again to see his calculated tactics so clearly. How he had chosen a fancy restaurant for their talk, a place so exclusive and formal he could almost be assured she wouldn't make a scene. As the maître d' had led them to their secluded, candle-lit table, Maura had thought Scott might even be planning to propose.

He had a little speech planned for her, all right, but it wasn't about marriage. Quite the opposite. Getting to know her the past six months had been great. Really fun, he'd said in a sympathetic tone. But the problem was, he'd be moving to Minnesota in a few weeks. He'd found a great job. Just what he'd been hoping for. She wouldn't want to hold him back, would she? Besides, they both knew this was a casual relationship. No strings. No expectations.

Then, ignoring her stunned expression, he'd patted her hand. Long-distance things never seemed to work out, he'd added, so it was best for both of them to end it now. To make a clean break. In a few weeks, he was sure, she'd thank him for making it so easy. She'd be happy she was free to meet someone new.

He hadn't waited for her answer. She was far too shocked at the time to make any reply at all.

It was right at that moment that she suddenly saw Scott differently, saw his true nature clearly. How had she been so blind? Was he that adept at misleading people? While she thought they were involved in a serious relationship—one that could lead to marriage—he'd merely been using her.

Maura felt a bitter taste at the memory. She touched her fingers to her eyes. She was crying. It seemed impossible that she had any tears left after the way she'd cried that night. She stopped walking and leaned against the wall of the corridor. Shaking her head to clear her thoughts, she reached into her pocket for a tissue.

"Maura?" She felt a touch on her shoulder and turned to see Doug Connelly's tall, commanding form beside her. "Are you all right?" he asked kindly.

"Uh…sure. I've just got something in my eye. A bit of dust or something," Maura mumbled. She pressed the tissue to her eye. "It will go away in a second."

"Here, let me see," Doug offered.

"No, really…it's okay," Maura murmured. But

before she could resist, he took her chin in his gentle grasp and turned her face up to the light.

His touch was firm but light, as she expected. He was a pediatric cardiologist, adept at putting his small patients at ease. His questioning gaze considered her troubled expression and she was sure he could see now that she'd lied to him. She was upset and crying, pure and simple.

"It looks as if it might be gone," he said quietly. His hand dropped away, but he continued to gaze down at her, his warm, amber eyes filled with concern.

They stood in a section of the hallway that was mostly glass, offering a courtyard view filled with trees, flowers and benches. Visitors and patients used it mainly, but some of the staff were outside, too, stealing a few minutes from their demanding jobs.

"What a day," Doug said. "Sometimes in this city, you feel like winter will never end. Then all of a sudden—bam. You look up and it's spring."

"Yes, spring did come suddenly this year." Maura looked out at the trees and flowers in full bloom. She'd been so depressed and distracted the past few weeks, she'd hardly noticed the changes.

"Let's get some fresh air. You look like you could use it." Doug took her arm without waiting for her reply.

"Thanks, but I really have to get back to the floor." Maura glanced at her watch, trying to excuse herself.

But Doug wouldn't let her leave his side so easily. "You can take a break for a few minutes, Maura. We'll cut across the courtyard and you can catch the elevators on the other side. That's closer to your station, anyway.''

Before Maura knew it, they were outside, walking down a tree-lined path. She felt the sunshine on her skin and inhaled the soft spring air. Doug had been right: she felt better almost instantly.

She glanced at his rugged profile and tall, lean form. He walked with his hands tucked into the pockets of his blue lab coat, his ever-present stethoscope slung around his neck, clearly enjoying a break in his hectic schedule. She had worked with many keenly intelligent doctors and many dedicated ones, as well, but she'd rarely met a physician who possessed both qualities in such abundance. Doug was more than dedicated. He was known as a bit of a workaholic, but he was an excellent physician. Maura was sure she knew none better. His powers of concentration and focus seemed evident even now, in his thoughtful expression and the firm set of his handsome features.

They strolled along in silence, side by side, but it was a comfortable silence for Maura. She had first come to know Doug as a colleague, when she'd been caring for one of his patients. After that, they'd quickly become friends. Especially after learning that Doug and Scott had gone to college together and had once been good friends. They'd been out of touch for years and had met again recently, when Scott came to work at Chicago General.

She often wondered how much Doug knew about her relationship with Scott and how close the two men were now. Scott always claimed he liked Doug, but often made cutting remarks about him. Maura could see Scott was simply jealous. He had once hoped to be a doctor, too, but had dropped out of medical school his first year. The same school from which Doug had graduated with honors.

While she wouldn't consider Doug a close friend, she had always felt a subtle but very strong connection to him. From the start they'd been able to talk to each other in an open, honest way. Which was quite unusual for Maura. She had always been shy with men, especially one so good-looking. But she rarely felt awkward with him. Something about him just put her at ease.

"Sit a minute," Doug suggested as they came to an empty bench.

"Sure." Maura shrugged and sat down. The bench was in the shade, facing a small fountain surrounded by flowers. The sound of the rippling water soothed her frazzled nerves, as did Doug's quiet, solid presence.

"Maura, what is it? What's troubling you?" Doug asked finally.

She turned to look at him. "What do you mean?"

"I know you were crying back there. And you look pale as a sheet."

Maura felt suddenly self-conscious under his scrutiny. She pushed a strand of wavy hair away from her face.

"I'm fine...I mean, I feel a little under the weather today. Just tired, I guess."

"Yes, you do look tired. You work too hard."

"Probably." She knew it was more like crying too hard—and sleeping too little.

Doug was quiet again for a moment. Then he said,

"Is this about Scott? Are you upset because he's leaving on Friday?"

"No. Not at all." She shook her head.

That was what everyone must think, she realized. That she was still yearning after a man who had treated her so badly. "Relieved is more like it," she added. "I wish he was already gone."

"He didn't deserve you." Doug's tone was firm and deep.

"That's nice of you to say," Maura replied quietly.

"I wasn't saying it to be nice. It's the truth." He paused, as if uncertain whether to continue. Then he said, "I know it feels awful, right now. But give it time. Before you know it, you'll forget all about him." He leaned toward her. "Maybe you should take some time off, get away for a while," he suggested.

"Yes, maybe I should," she replied vaguely. Last night she had thought about visiting her sister on the West Coast, the only real family she had left. But she knew very well that no matter how fast or how far she ran, she could never escape this problem.

She turned and looked at him and could see he was sincerely worried about her. The look in his eye, the sheer kindness and consideration, was her undoing. She had been on an emotional roller coaster the past twenty-four hours, and having Doug, of all people, look at her that way made her feel as if she was about to burst into tears again.

She felt the moisture well up in her eyes and dropped her face into her hands. Then she felt Doug's strong arm circle her shoulders as hot tears streamed down her cheeks. Doug pulled her closer, his grip strong and warm around her, his chest firm under her cheek. She was crying hard, sobbing uncontrollably, unable to stop herself.

"It's okay," she heard him murmur against her hair.

She tried to speak and felt a giant lump in her throat again. No, it's not okay, she wanted to say. It's anything but.

"Just cry if you need to," Doug whispered.

"Oh, Doug...I'm sorry. I just don't know what to do...."

Her voice trailed off in another wave of tears and she pressed her face against his hard chest.

She felt Doug's strong hand stroking her hair. She felt the warmth of his body and breathed in the scent of his skin. With her eyes closed and her cheek nestled in the crook of his shoulder, she felt safe and protected. For the briefest moment, Maura allowed herself the lovely fantasy that she could stay this way forever. How much easier everything would be.

But that was impossible. She had to pull herself together. There was no one to help her out of this mess. Doug might offer his strong shoulder to cry on, but he didn't have a white charger standing by for a quick getaway. He was only trying to be a good friend.

She took a deep breath and forced herself to move away from his embrace.

"I'm sorry. I didn't mean to upset you by talking about Scott," Doug apologized.

"It wasn't that." She wiped her eyes and took a shaky breath. She felt him watching her, waiting for her to speak.

Finally, she said, "It's just that I have this problem...." She paused again and staring straight ahead, she admitted, "I'm pregnant."

She wasn't sure why she'd told him. The words spoken aloud sounded so final. So overwhelming. Doug looked shocked for an instant. Then he quickly hid his reaction, she noticed. He was silent for a long moment, and she watched as his pensive expression grew harsher. Angrier.

"With Scott's child," he said.

Though it wasn't a question, she nodded and looked away again.

He leaned forward and pushed his hand through his thick hair. "Does he know?"

"I told him a few minutes ago. In his office. That's why I looked upset in the hall," she admitted.

"He didn't take the news very well, I guess," Doug replied sternly.

"No. He didn't."

The ugly scene replayed in her mind, and suddenly she couldn't bear talking about it anymore.

"Listen, thanks for talking to me," she said as she stood to go. "But I'd better get back to work. I've already been gone way too long."

"I understand." He nodded and came to his feet. "Maybe I'll see you later, when I do rounds."

"Sure. And I'm sorry for crying all over you." He must see her as some kind of flailing, helpless female, she thought, when in fact, she was just the opposite.

"Don't even think about it, Maura." His tone was soft and sincere. Maura met his gaze briefly, then turned on her way.

She hurried across the courtyard, then entered the

hospital. To avoid the long wait for the elevator, she walked up three flights to the pediatrics department. Her supervisor, Gloria Jones, greeted her with a questioning look but didn't ask why she was so late returning from her break. There was plenty of work waiting, and Maura dug in, eager to focus on her patients instead of her problems.

As the afternoon passed, her thoughts returned to her disturbing confrontation with Scott—and her conversation with Dr. Connelly. She'd never had such a personal conversation with Doug before. But now she was thankful that, purely by chance, he'd been there for her at such an awful moment. Crying on his shoulder hadn't solved anything, but it had made her feel worlds better, lending her the boost she needed to carry on.

Some of the staff disliked the handsome pediatrician. They found him aloof and distant. But Maura had never felt that way. He was sometimes distracted by his work, and even brooding. But a more dedicated doctor would be hard to find.

She had never imagined he would also be such a dedicated friend, the kind you could really count on when things went haywire. But whether you liked Doug Connelly or not, he was clearly a man of strong character, and Maura knew without question that her secret was safe.

Her workday wore on, thankfully free of pressing emergencies, as she had a pounding headache that wasn't assuaged by the pills she'd taken earlier. Luckily, a night-shift nurse came in early, allowing Maura to go home.

She lived in a comfortable family neighborhood a

short distance from the hospital. She'd been lucky to find a reasonably priced two-bedroom apartment in a renovated brownstone. Her living room even had a working fireplace, which she really appreciated during the long Chicago winters.

The apartment was the first she'd lived in without a roommate, and Maura had loved decorating it to her own taste. She liked antiques, but since she could only afford a few small pieces, she used her knack for finding interesting items that weren't genuine antiques but still quaint and unique. The honey-tone wood floors were covered by area rugs, and the walls were warm shades of apricot and creamy white. Her home was her haven, her retreat from her hectic, demanding job. It was a private place where she could rest and recharge. Where she could hide away and sort out her thoughts when life tossed her some seemingly impossible crisis. Which was just the way she felt tonight as she slipped her key into the front door and went inside.

She dropped her mail on a table in the foyer without even glancing at it, then went straight to the bedroom and took a long, hot shower. Even though it was still early, she put on her nightgown and robe, then lay down on her bed, hoping to sleep. But worries immediately crowded her mind.

For some reason, instead of thinking about Scott, she thought about Doug, recalling the first time they'd met, months ago. She had recently started at the hospital and had been working the night shift. She was assigned to one of his patients, a four-year-old girl brought in with advanced pneumonia and serious heart complications. Purely by chance in the small hours of the night she'd discovered that the child was in serious trouble, in danger of heart failure.

When Doug found her with the patient minutes later, she was giving CPR as she waited for the crash cart and respiratory equipment to be hooked up. As Doug took charge, he barely said a personal word to her, but the respectful, grateful look in his eyes said it all.

That night she'd hardly been aware of his compelling good looks, or the smothering shyness that typically fell over her. Working through the crisis with him, she felt totally in synch, and the event somehow forged a mysterious but deep bond between them. She had never felt quite that way about anyone—not a co-worker or even a romantic partner. But she had felt it that night with Doug, and forever after.

They had worked together for several hours to pull the little girl through. Even after Maura's regular shift was done, she stayed on, unwilling to leave until she was sure the child was going to survive. She knew that some people thought it unwise to get so involved with each patient's recovery. They advised compassion tempered by a cooler, more distant attitude to avoid the burnout that was so common among overworked nurses.

But Maura wasn't made that way. She hadn't become a pediatric nurse in order to be distant and detached from the children who needed her. She knew from the first that Doug was the same. Perhaps even more intensely involved with his young patients than she.

She later learned that the little girl's family didn't have much insurance and Doug had not even sent them a bill. While it was highly uncommon for a specialist of Doug's caliber to forego payment, she soon learned that it wasn't uncommon at all for him to work that way.

When morning came and the crisis had passed, she and Doug sat together outside on a bench in the same courtyard where they had talked today. They celebrated their victory, joking and laughing over cups of steaming coffee and sticky donuts. It was late January and the weather was frigid, yet she could still recall feeling elated by the cold air and early-morning light and the shared success in saving a child's life.

It was then Doug learned she was dating Scott Walker, and Maura learned Doug was Scott's old pal from college. There was something in Doug's reaction to the news that made Maura think he was disappointed to hear she was seeing someone. But the moment passed and later she decided she'd imagined the brief flicker of interest.

On her side Maura would never deny that she found Doug very attractive. But at that time she had felt so committed to Scott, she'd never once thought of Doug in a romantic way.

Besides, Maura reflected, even if she had been free, Doug was not her type at all. For one thing, she was looking for a man who would have time in his life for a wife and family. Doug was far too focused on his work to make family life, or even a romantic relationship, a priority.

And he could be temperamental at times. She had to acknowledge that his smiles and bright moods were rare. He seemed most often to be shadowed by some deep, mysterious unhappiness, and too often she found a dark, brooding look in his eyes when he thought no one was watching him.

What brought on that somber mood of his? Was it the pressures of his work? Maura had always suspected it was something more. Some deep hurt in his past, some painful loss. Doug had never spoken to her about his past, but she did know from Scott that he'd gone through a difficult divorce a few years back.

As the months passed, she and Doug always had so much to say to each other whenever they met. She'd run into him on her floor while he did rounds, in the hallways, in the cafeteria. He would ask her advice about his cases, and she enjoyed helping him figure out some knotty problem in a diagnosis or discuss a curious turn in a patient's condition.

It was unusual for a doctor of his standing to take a nurse into his confidence in that way, and she was secretly pleased, even proud, of the way he seemed to value her observations. But they didn't only talk about patients. They talked about all kinds of things, movies, books, traveling to exotic places, which they both planned on doing someday when they weren't working so hard.

But Maura had to acknowledge that, for all their interesting conversations, she still knew very little about him. The staff at Chicago General was always brimming with gossip, and while she avoided discussing other people's lives, she had overheard a few basic facts about Doug. He had been at the hospital since his residency and at one time had been married. He was divorced for almost two years, but no one seemed to know what had gone wrong. His ex-wife was now married to a prominent plastic surgeon, and some said she'd hurt Doug badly with an affair.

Even though she didn't have romantic designs on him herself, Maura wondered why he wasn't in a new relationship, or even married again, by now. But her knowledgeable co-workers answered that question, too. Many hopeful women had pursued the handsome doctor, but the relationship had always ended unhappily. Despite his giving, caring nature as a physician, it was reported that Dr. Douglas Connelly was distant and even difficult as a romantic partner. An emotional Mount Everest with wickedly icy heights to scale.

Maura suspected his single-minded focus on his work had been the real problem. She knew it would be one for her. Some people didn't need a home life and family. Maybe Doug was that type, she concluded. But a home and family was something Maura had always longed for, because she'd known so little security growing up.

When she'd met Scott, back in November, she'd believed at last she'd found a man who shared her values and outlook and wanted the same kind of life that she did.

Her thoughts drifted as sleep overcame her weary mind. How devastating it had been to discover that Scott had only pretended to be that kind of man, saying just what she'd wanted to hear in order to get what he'd wanted from her.

And by the time she saw him clearly, it was too late.

Two

Maura woke to the sound of sharp knocking on her front door. Her bedroom was dark, and the clock on the night table showed it was nearly eight. She sat up and pushed her hair back with her hand as she walked toward the foyer.

She wondered who it could be. Maybe her friend Liza, who lived downstairs. Liza often stopped by at night just to chat, mostly about her problems with boyfriends.

But Maura wasn't in the mood to see Liza. She walked toward the door and tightened the sash on her robe, wondering what excuse she could make.

Just as the knock sounded again, Maura turned the lock. "Just a second," she said.

She pulled the door open a space. Then felt herself jolted to the core by the sight of Doug's tall, imposing form.

"Doug. What are you doing here?"

She was rarely so blunt, but he was that last person she'd expected. He'd only been to her apartment once, when her car wouldn't start and he'd given her a lift home from the hospital. She didn't even realize he remembered where she lived.

"I was on my way home and thought I'd stop by. I went to your station after my rounds, but they said you'd left early," he added. "I hope you're all right."

He smiled at her, yet his gaze looked serious, questioning, as if he wasn't sure he'd done the right thing by surprising her like this.

"Another nurse came in early, so I was able to leave before the shift ended," she explained. "I was just taking a nap."

"Have you had dinner yet? We could get something at the café around the corner if you like."

"Thanks, but I think I'd rather stay in tonight. I mean, I appreciate you stopping over—"

"That's all right. But I did want to talk to you some more. You seemed so upset today. I'm not sure it's good for you to be alone."

"I-I'm okay," she insisted. "Really." But she wasn't okay and they both knew it.

"Maura?" Doug moved up to the opening in the door, his tone firm but concerned. "Please, let me in. I'll only stay a minute."

She took a deep breath. Then, without saying anything more, she stepped back and let him in. He was probably right. It wasn't good for her to be alone right now. She might feel better if she talked to him for a while. He knew Scott and he seemed so understanding about her problem. Maybe he could help her sort things out.

She closed the door and they stood facing each other. A small lamp on a side table cast the foyer in soft, golden light. Shadows emphasized his strong features, his wide, firm mouth and amber eyes.

She suddenly felt self-conscious dressed in just her bathrobe, but there was no help for it. She knew she looked a mess, her hair hanging in wild waves down past her shoulders and her eyes circled with shadows. She met his steady gaze, then looked away, tucking a strand of hair behind her ear.

"I know you're tired. I won't stay long," he promised.

"It's okay. I'm glad you're here." It was true, she realized. She met his gaze, then looked away. "Let's go into the living room."

She led the way and sat on the couch. Doug stood a short distance away, his brows drawn together in a frown. She suddenly wondered about the thoughts causing that dark look. Did he think badly of her, that she was not very particular or careful about her romantic partners? The irony was, if anything, it was her naiveté and lack of experience with men that had gotten her into this fix. But of course Doug wouldn't know that, and she felt foolish trying to explain it to him, certain he'd think she was making excuses for herself.

Doug turned and sat down in the armchair across from her. "You never really told me what Scott said to you about the baby. Only that he reacted badly."

She sighed and gripped her hands in her lap. "We didn't part on the best terms. I basically haven't spoken to him since he broke up with me and announced he was leaving for Minnesota. When I went to see him today, to tell him about the baby, he offered to pay for an abortion...but that was all.''

"That bastard." Doug's eyes glinted with anger. "Is that all he said to you? He didn't say he'd help you through the pregnancy or support his own child?"

Maura had wanted to avoid relating the uglier details of the conversation, but now she decided to tell Doug all.

"No, just the opposite, actually. He said that if I had the child, it would be my responsibility and I'd have to take him to court before he'd share in any financial support. He also said he hoped I wouldn't make a big deal out of this. It would be bad for my career and for his, and he hoped that I'd...I'd be smart and do the right thing."

"He said that?" Doug rose to his feet, his fists balled as if he wanted to strike something or someone. "I'd like to do the right thing to him...that smug, self-righteous son of a—"

Maura had never seen Doug this angry. His powerful emotions frightened her. Was it due to some long-standing enmity or rivalry between him and Scott? A tension Scott had sometimes hinted about. Or was he simply angry on her behalf?

"Doug, please. I really don't care if Scott's involved. I did believe I was in love with him at one time," she admitted, "but now I can see I was in some fantasyland. I never really knew him."

Doug turned to her again, and she thought her words had taken some of the edge off his anger.

"I was shocked at first by his reaction," she continued. "But maybe it's a good thing that he wants no connection to me or the baby. With any luck I'll never have anything to do with him again."

He paced across the room, then suddenly turned to face her.

"Yes, I guess you're right. You're certainly better off without him," he admitted in a calmer tone. "And my confronting him wouldn't help matters, would it?"

"Not at all," she assured him.

"Except to make me feel a hell of a lot better," he added, more to himself than to Maura. He took a deep breath and she could see him willing himself to cool off.

"Sorry, Maura. This doesn't help you any." He shook his head then glanced down at her. "Have you decided what you're going to do?"

He'd asked the question quietly, almost casually. Yet she sensed him focusing on her reply with laser-like intensity. Not just the way a friend would be interested, but as if the matter somehow affected him directly, as well.

"I want to keep my baby," she said firmly. "I have to."

"I knew you would say that." Doug's expression softened, and a warm light glowed in his eyes as he gazed at her. "But raising a child on your own will be hard. Harder than you think," he said knowingly. "My mother was a single parent. She didn't even have family to help her. She really did it all on her own. With twin boys, no less," he added. "Until I was an adult, I never even understood or appreciated how much she had to deal with. Sometimes I know I can never fully appreciate it, either.''

Maura had not known that Doug had been raised only by his mother. It couldn't have been easy for him growing up. The accomplishment of completing medical school seemed even more impressive now. He was right. It wouldn't be an easy road for her or her child.

''I know what you're saying. I've thought about this—the problems I'll face. But I can't see it any other way. I just can't put the child up for adoption,'' she added. It was hard to continue, but she forced herself. Now it was her turn to reveal some hidden part of her history. ''I know what it's like to be part of a family...but not really part of it. It's a terrible, lonely feeling. Like you're always on the outside looking in,'' she added quietly, remembering unhappier times.

''I'd rather raise my child alone and give it all the love one parent can give than sit and wonder, every day, if my baby is happy and cared for.''

''You were adopted?'' he asked.

She shook her head. ''A foster child, from the time I was about twelve years old. Both my parents died in a car accident. My sister and I had no close relatives to raise us. We were split up and sent to different foster homes. Some of the people were nice to me. They wanted to help and tried to make me feel a part of their family. But there were always problems. I never stayed anywhere for very long,'' she confided wistfully. ''Then I managed to get a scholarship to college and started living on my own.''

''How sad to lose both your parents so young,'' he

said gravely. "At least I always had my mother and brother. You never mentioned your family before. I had no idea."

"Yes, well, you never mentioned yours either," she said. "We've never talked much about personal things like this before, have we?"

"No, we haven't. But maybe it's long past time that we did."

He glanced at her briefly as he sat down on the other end of the couch, crossing one long leg over the other and stretching out his arm along the back of the sofa. Despite his size, he moved gracefully, Maura noticed, with a powerful masculine grace that was distracting to her.

"Considering all you've been through, Maura, I'd think you would have turned out differently somehow."

"Differently? How do you mean?"

"I'm not sure exactly. Not nearly as optimistic for one thing. And you're such a caring, giving person."

His thoughtful words lifted her spirits and, more than that, made her remember who she was and what she was capable of.

"I had a good start, I guess. I had two parents who loved their children and loved each other. We lived in a small town in Wisconsin, just outside of Madison. It was really an ideal childhood, you might say." She looked down for a moment and gathered her thoughts. "Sometimes when I think about my family life back then, I think it might be unfair to the baby to raise it on my own. I know that there are decent, good people out there who would give an adopted child lots of love and a wonderful home. And sometimes I do feel scared to do this on my own.''

She felt her throat tighten with emotion, making it hard to continue. She didn't want to start crying again but felt the tears well up in her eyes. ''I don't know…I just feel so confused, so overwhelmed,'' she admitted in a shaky voice.

Doug touched her shoulder. He seemed about to speak, then stopped himself. She could see he was giving her a moment to calm herself and collect her thoughts again.

It was still hard for Maura to believe she was pregnant.

How could she begin to explain it to Doug, when she herself hardly understood how this happened? To her, of all people? She'd always felt that physical intimacy between a man and a woman was a serious step, part of a relationship that included love and commitment. Even so, she had little experience that way and had always been so careful.

But Scott had had a way of sweeping aside her doubts and Maura had believed that she loved him. She had thought herself so lucky that a successful, good-looking man like Scott had wanted her. She couldn't understand what had attracted him to a mousy little thing like her. She couldn't help it, but that was how she thought of herself. She knew she wasn't attractive and sexy like some of the women around the hospital. She was quite the opposite, the type people used to call a plain Jane, feeling most comfortable when she blended into the woodwork. Sometimes friends like Liza insisted that she had what it took to turn heads, if she would only play up her looks a bit. But Maura always thought they were just trying to be nice. She could never quite believe it.

Maybe she felt safer downplaying her looks. As a teenager, just starting to blossom, she'd had some bad experiences attracting the wrong kind of male attention—the clumsy and crass advances of boys and even adult men in her foster families. She had learned to put as little emphasis as possible on her appearance. In her heart she hoped that the right man would be attracted to what was inside, not to some pretty packaging.

That was part of the reason she thought Scott might be the right man for her. Plain Jane or not, Scott pursued her and wooed her, and she was very flattered by his attentions. While he sometimes acted thoughtlessly in a way that was hurtful to her, he always managed to win her back again. It was hard to stay mad at him when he turned on the charm.

She knew he had his faults. But didn't everybody? Maura didn't expect the man she married to be perfect. She had so little experience when it came to romance that she hardly knew what to expect. No wonder she now found herself in this situation.

She shook her head as if to clear her muddled thoughts, then glanced over at Doug. Their eyes met, his golden gaze full of concern for her. For her future and her baby's, she thought.

She unconsciously touched her hand to her stomach, which was still perfectly flat. Yet she imagined the new life growing there, minute by minute, hour by hour.

"I've been thinking I might leave Chicago. It's hard to raise a child here."

"Leave Chicago?" Doug's expression darkened. "Where would you go?"

"Maybe to Portland, to be near my sister, Ellen. Or maybe to Santa Fe. I have a good friend from school there. I might be better off someplace new, making a fresh start."

"I don't think that's a good idea at all, Maura," Doug said sternly. He abruptly got up off the couch and paced across the room again, looking almost as disturbed as he'd been hearing about her talk with Scott.

"It'll be difficult and stressful to start a new job and get settled in a new city," he pointed out. "What if the pregnancy doesn't go well? You'd be all alone, with no one to help you."

But she was all alone now, here in Chicago, Maura wanted to say. But she didn't want Doug to think she felt sorry for herself. She really didn't.

"I'm confused, I guess. What do you think I should do?" she asked, her eyes wide and questioning.

He stared at her a long time, making Maura feel suddenly very aware of being alone with him. She thought he was about to say something, then saw the firm set of his mouth as he mentally backtracked.

"I think there's a lot to sort out. But it sounds like you've made the most important decision of all. To keep the baby," he said. He sat down on the couch again next to her, their bodies close but not touching. "I'm not sure you can figure out much more to-night."

He was right. She was exhausted and it was hard to think clearly.

"I guess you're right. I can't figure out my entire

future in five minutes.'' She sighed and glanced over at him. ''But thanks again for listening. It's really helped me,'' she said sincerely.

''I want to help you any way I can, Maura. I mean it,'' he promised her.

The emotion in his voice surprised her, and before she could answer, he shifted over on the couch, closing the small space between them. He put his arm around her shoulder and held her close.

His nearness was a soothing balm to her soul. They didn't talk for a few moments, and Maura allowed herself to simply relax and soak up the strength and comfort he offered.

After a time she said, ''What really made you come here tonight?''

''Just what I said when I came in, I was worried about you and thought you could use some company.''

She honestly hadn't realized that Doug thought about her as much as he apparently did. Maybe he didn't think of her in a romantic way, but their relationship did seem to matter to him, she reflected.

Then he shifted and glanced down at her and she knew intuitively there was something more. Something he was reluctant to say.

''Look, I know this sounds crazy, but I feel like this is partly my fault. This problem of yours, I mean.'' She felt his broad chest expand as he took a deep breath. ''I've known Scott a very long time. I know how he treats women. I wasn't surprised at all when I heard about the way he broke up with you,'' he admitted. ''Months ago, when I first met you and learned you were seeing him, I thought about saying something to you. To warn you in some way about him. But I didn't want to interfere. I could see you really cared for him and he seemed to care for you. You seemed happy together," he added, sounding almost angry to admit it, Maura noticed. Though she couldn't understand why.

"Was I happy? Yes, at first I guess I was," she agreed. "Until I really got to know him."

"I'd hoped that maybe you would figure him out sooner than most, and get through it without any serious damage. But it didn't turn out that way, I guess," Doug said. "Does it bother you to hear these things about him?" he added.

Maura shook her head. "No, not at all. In a strange way it makes me feel better. When Scott broke up with me, I felt it was all my fault. As if there was some reason I couldn't make him love me and want to stay with me. Now I can see that it wasn't me at all."

"No, not you at all, Maura. Scott would have been lucky beyond deserving if he'd made a commitment to you," Doug assured her. "Still, I feel responsible for how things ended up. If I had told you about Scott, about his past, maybe this would never have happened."

Maura was stunned by his line of reasoning. She pulled back and stared up at him. "Don't be ridiculous. I'd never make that connection in a million years."

"I know you don't see it that way. But I do," he argued. "I knew you were too good for him. I knew how he'd end things with you. Just like all the others. I should have warned you."

"Even if you had, I wouldn't have believed you or taken your advice to heart," Maura replied honestly. "I really thought we were in love and that Scott wanted to marry me someday."

"Maybe you wouldn't have listened to me. Not at first. But it might have helped you see his true colors sooner," he added somberly.

Maura met his gaze. Perhaps that was true. But what good did it do to wonder about that now? She had to deal with the present and figure out some plan for the future.

"It doesn't matter. Let's not argue about it," she urged him. "The point is, I'm the only one responsible for dating Scott…and for everything that happened after."

She rose abruptly, then instantly felt her head spin. Doug was beside her in a split second, his arm wrapped tightly around her waist.

"Maura, are you dizzy?"

"Just a little. I haven't eaten much today," she realized. "That must be it."

He piled up some couch pillows so she could lie back comfortably. "Here, rest a minute. I'll fix you something."

"You don't have to do that," she said. "I can manage."

"I said rest," he ordered in a stern tone. "I'm the doctor, remember?"

When she looked up at him in surprise, he flashed a sexy, stubborn grin.

"Okay, okay. You win." She sat back with a sigh and a small smile. "I didn't know you could cook, Dr. Connelly," she added curiously.

"Me? I'm great in the kitchen—if you like scrambled eggs and toast."

Maura laughed for the first time in days.

"Eggs on the dry side, please. Just a little jelly on the toast," she replied as her head sunk back into the pillows.

"You got it." He leaned over and covered her with a throw, then strolled off to the kitchen.

Maura felt her eyes close, her scattered thoughts lulled by the sounds and tempting smells of Doug's cooking and the powerful, calming force of his presence. For the first time in days she felt some tranquillity and some hope about the future.

Her hands floated protectively to her stomach and she thought about her baby. During all her shock and worry, the single most important element in all this had been obscured, she realized. She was honestly thrilled to be expecting a child, no matter what the circumstances.

When Doug had asked about her intentions, she hadn't revealed half of her true feelings about the baby. The truth was she wanted this child more than anything. Becoming pregnant made her see that she was very much alone in the world. Maybe she had always wanted a child, to love and be loved by the one person in her life who would always belong to her. She had a good relationship with her sister, but Ellen lived in Portland and had a family of her own. Maura had no one truly close.

Since her parents' tragic accident and the trauma of watching her family fall to pieces, Maura had been on a private journey, longing to return to that special place of warmth, love and security she had known as a child. She had imagined creating that kind of stable, loving home life as part of a traditional marriage. But it hadn't happened that way. Now she had to play the cards she'd been dealt. Despite her worries and fears, in her heart she was grateful for the new life growing inside of her.

She loved her baby already and knew that she would do her utmost to give her child a good life, to give him or her all the love, security and happiness that a child deserves.

Even if she had to do it all on her own. It would work out somehow, she told herself. It would.

Eggs, milk and butter. A bowl, a frying pan and toaster. Doug easily found what he needed and set to work on Maura's dinner. Their conversation had left him all stirred up, as emotionally scrambled as the bowl of beaten eggs in his hand, and he was glad to focus on some practical task, like cooking. He poured the eggs in the pan, then glanced out into the living room. Maura lay with her eyes closed, and he wondered if she'd fallen asleep. Just as well, he thought. She needed a break. And so did he, to sort out his thoughts about all this.

He felt bad for her, even partly responsible for the fix she was in. He truly wanted to help her, to do what he could. Doug knew that everything he'd just told Maura was true. But he also knew that there was one reaction to her news he had not disclosed. A gut response even stronger than all the rest.

He wanted a baby. He'd wanted one for a very long time. It was the real reason his marriage had fallen apart, and after that disaster his chances of being a father seemed even farther out of reach.

After his divorce, he just couldn't seem to let any woman close enough for a serious relationship. He'd had that once, and once was enough. Romance was for movies and books, as far as he could see. People only fooled themselves into thinking those earth-shaking hormonal rushes were true love. After the tornado died down, there was only disappointment and pain.

So how would he ever be a father? Unless he got some woman pregnant by "accident," as Scott had done to Maura. But that would never be Doug's style.

He put two slices of bread into the toaster, then jammed it down with a bit more force than necessary. The news of Maura's pregnancy and Scott's reaction had felt like salt poured into an open wound. He cursed Scott for the way he'd treated her, and felt an even deeper bitterness for the way the man had turned his back on his child. Doug felt his jaw grow rigid as the anger swelled in him all over again. If a woman like Maura had come to him with news like that, it would have been the happiest day of his life. Why was life so unfair sometimes?

Doug scooped the cooked eggs onto a plate, then spread some jelly on the toast. He grabbed a fork and napkin, then headed out to the living room. But even before he reached the couch he could see that Maura was fast asleep. She looked so peaceful, as if she didn't have a care in the world. He didn't have the heart to wake her. Watching her sleep, he felt another wave of sympathy for her. She was such a good person. A wonderful person, truly. He really couldn't remember knowing a woman he liked or respected more. She didn't deserve Scott's mistreatment. She didn't deserve to face such an overwhelming problem all alone. But what could he do to help her? Stand by her as her friend? Give her money maybe, if she'd let him? There didn't seem much he could do. And what if she moved away? What then? They would lose touch and he'd never see her again. Or her baby.

The possibility upset him. He almost had the urge to wake her and get her to talk some more about her plans. Instead he set the dish of eggs on the coffee table, then sat down to wait.

Maura's eyes opened slowly. Doug's face, very close to her own, filled her field of vision. His golden eyes glittered in the shadowy light, rugged features tempered by a slight smile. She stared up at him, studying the strong lines of his brow and chin, his amber eyes, square jaw and wide, soft mouth.

Then he lifted his hand and softly pushed a lock of her hair off her cheek…and she knew she wasn't dreaming. This was real. Too real for her peace of mind.

"I'm sorry. I didn't mean to fall asleep again," she murmured.

"Better get used to it. Pregnant women fall asleep at the drop of a hat," he reported with a slight smile. "Your scrambled eggs got cold. But you looked so peaceful, I didn't have the heart to wake you."

He was seated on the edge of the couch near her hip and leaning over her. His gaze met hers, and she couldn't look away, feeling only vaguely aware of the movement of his hand, as it came to rest on the curve of her waist. Maura thought to sit up and move away, but she felt frozen in place. She felt as if everything was suddenly moving at a superslow pace. Even her words seemed delayed as she tried to speak.

"It must be late," she said finally.

Doug made no move to check his watch, and she wondered if he had even heard her. His gaze moved slowly over her face, studying her, feature by feature, as if seeing her for the very first time.

"You probably ought to go," she whispered.

"Probably," he replied in a low, husky tone. His hand moved from her hair to cup her cheek, and before Maura could utter a single word, his mouth met hers in a deep, hungry kiss.

The touch of his lips to hers started out as a sensual savoring. Maura's senses reeled with pleasure. All logical thought was totally short-circuited as Doug's supple lips teased and tasted, coaxing her full response. Her hands automatically rose up to his strong shoulders, and the feel of his firm muscles and warm skin under fingertips instantly melted her last resistance.

She made a small moan in the back of her throat, a sound of half pleasure, half surrender.

She felt his response as his arms moved tightly around her, his kiss growing deeper. Their passion accelerated instantly, from zero to one hundred in a millisecond. It was as if a mysterious switch, hidden somewhere deep inside, had been flipped. Her mouth opened easily under his probing tongue, and her arms wound around his powerful shoulders. She felt him move next to her on the couch and she shifted over, so that he stretched out next to her, their legs and arms and tongues entwined.

The kiss that had begun so tenderly grew bolder. Hungry and intense. A knockout sensual punch that sent Maura's senses spinning.

His embrace tightened as his tongue plunged into her mouth, sliding seductively against her own. His large, strong hands glided down her satin-covered back, sweeping over her waist and hips, then down to cup her bottom, pulling her close to his heat.

Then his warm lips left her mouth and wandered in a scintillating path down the column of her throat. His hand glided up over her soft curves and gently cupped her throbbing breast.

What was happening here? she wondered vaguely as she kissed him back. For all the months and all the intimacy she'd shared with Scott, he had never once kissed her like this.

No one had ever kissed her like this.

And never once had she felt this way in any man's arms. So vibrantly alive, so sensual, so uninhibited.

Then suddenly, as if remembering himself, Doug lifted his head. "Maura…" he murmured in surprise. He dropped his head against her shoulder and took a deep breath. "I shouldn't have done that," he admitted in a harsh whisper.

Then, with some effort, he pulled away and pulled her robe up to cover her shoulders. "I came here to help you, not cause more problems."

"I know that," Maura said. She believed it, too.

Still, she felt shaken. Shaken to the core. His merest touch had sent her up in flames. She suddenly realized with a shock the strong attraction they shared.

An attraction that she had so far been basically unaware of.

He sat up and took another long breath, then glanced at her with an awestruck expression. Then he got up and walked across the room as if he truly needed to put some space between them. He stood with his back to her, his hands on his hips.

Maura sat up, too, and fumbled with her robe. She wondered what he was thinking. Probably he was just plain confused. She felt confused, as well. One minute Doug was her pal, her surrogate big brother, and the next minute…

Well, to be perfectly honest, she always knew there was a spark on her side, but she'd been committed to Scott and never even dared explore those feelings. Besides, she only once had the slightest hint that Doug felt drawn to her that way. Did he have feelings for her that he'd never revealed because she was not free?

Then again, they had never been alone like this before, in such an intimate situation. An emotional tinderbox. That was it right there, she decided. Things like this can happen to people in a crisis. He'd just been swept away by the circumstances. He was feeling sorry for her, maybe even protective.

All these emotions had gotten confused in his mind. In her mind, too. It didn't mean anything. She couldn't allow herself to think that one kiss—one mind-blowing kiss, she had to admit—signaled something more.

Finally he turned to her, his handsome features calm and composed. She willed herself to act the same.

He looked about to speak, but she cut in before he could say a word. "That's okay. Don't even say it."

His thick brows drew together in a frown. "How do you know what I was going to say?"

"I just know," she replied. "You're sorry you kissed me. You didn't really mean it. These things happen. And you hope that it doesn't change our friendship. Right?"

He stared at her with a narrowed gaze. "Wrong," he said firmly. "I'm not the least bit sorry I kissed you. Surprised, maybe, and hoping you don't think I was trying to take advantage of you. But definitely not sorry."

"You're not?"

"Heaven knows, I didn't mean for it to happen like that, but it's probably just as well. It makes the next thing I want to say easier."

She was confused again. Had she missed something? "The next thing? Which is…?"

"Which is," he said slowly, drawing the word out in his deep, low voice, "that I've figured out what you should do."

He walked slowly toward her, and Maura felt her heartbeat quicken at the strange, unsettling light in his eye. Inner warning bells sounded. She couldn't put her finger on it, but she felt something was about to happen to her.

Something momentous and totally unexpected.

He was standing right in front of her now, his muscular arms crossed over his broad chest. She had to tilt her head back to look up at him. Her mouth felt dry as she started to speak.

"And what do you think that is?" she asked in a halting tone.

"Simple." His low, commanding tone gave her chills. "Marry me."

"Marry you?" Maura wasn't sure she'd heard him correctly. She couldn't believe he was proposing to her.

"That's what I said. I'm asking you to marry me," he repeated patiently, holding her wide-eyed gaze.

"But how can I marry you?" She knew the question sounded silly as soon as she spoke the words, but she was too stunned to edit her reaction. "I mean, our relationship...we're just friends. I can't just marry you."

She saw him blink, yet his expression showed no other reaction. She unconsciously bit her lip and looked away.

"A husband and wife *should* be friends," he replied smoothly. "Don't you think?"

"Of course I do. It's just that there has to be something more to it."

"Like love, you mean?" His deep voice held an uncharacteristically cynical note. "Let me tell you something, Maura. People get married every day thinking they're totally, wildly, unbelievably in love. And more than half of them end up having rotten marriages."

"Yes," she said quietly. She tucked a strand of hair behind her ear. "I'm sure that's true."

He was referring to his own failed marriage, no doubt, and she was curious to hear more. Yet she could tell it was still a painful topic and she didn't think it was the time to ask him about it.

"I know you think this sounds crazy," he continued. "I thought the same, too, when I first had the idea. But I've had some time to think it through while you were dozing," he gently teased her. "I know this could work. I feel it in my gut. I respect you. I care for you. We share the same values and understand the demands of the kind of work we both do. We both love children. And you even laugh at my bad jokes," he added with a smile.

"Only because I don't want to hurt your feelings. I know how thin-skinned doctors can be," she returned with a grin.

He laughed, and she met his warm gaze.

He really was so handsome. Even more so than usual right now, with that persuasive, hopeful expression on his face. And she knew that he was a decent man. Kind, even noble. Intelligent and successful, as well.

Any woman in her right mind would want to marry him, a little voice inside urged. But could she possibly go through with such a thing? They barely knew each other. They certainly weren't in love. Although after that kiss, there could be little question about physical compatibility...

No, she didn't dare think that far. Besides, even if they went through with it, he'd said nothing about it being a *real* marriage.

Still, as she glanced at him again, she felt her resistance melting away second by second. If he persisted in this amazing proposal, where would she ever find the strength to refuse him?

"I understand what you're saying, Doug. I feel the same about you...and I appreciate your offering to help me. Honestly,'' she added, meeting his gaze for an instant. ''But how can I marry you? I really can't.''

''Of course you can,'' he insisted in a quiet but firm tone. ''You absolutely can.''

''But it's not fair to you. You may regret it. I'm almost sure you will.''

''I won't regret it, Maura. I swear to you.'' His tone was utterly solemn and final, and his gaze held hers steadily.

She didn't answer. She just couldn't. She looked away, clenching her hands in her lap. ''I...I just don't know what to say.''

He walked over to where she sat, crouched down beside her and took hold of both of her hands, enfolding them gently in his own. ''Maura, I understand your doubts, I really do. But, believe me, I really want to marry you. I want to make a home with you and be a father to your baby. At least let's try. Look, let's make a deal. What if we agree to stay married until the baby comes. If you're not happy after that, we'll figure out what to do.''

Maura couldn't speak for a moment. She couldn't take her eyes away from his. She took a deep breath and prayed to heaven that she would do the right thing.

''For the baby. Maybe you're right,'' she finally said.

Doug smiled into her eyes. ''Does that mean you're saying yes?''

Maura stared straight ahead. Her heart was pounding so hard she was sure he could hear it. Could this really be happening to her?

She turned to him and touched her hand to his lean

cheek. "Yes, I'd be honored to marry you," she said quietly, the words just about sticking in her throat. "And I agree to your deal. If either of us wants out of the marriage after the baby comes, there'll be no questions asked."

"Good," he said simply, his voice so low and deep it made her shudder.

What in heaven's name was she doing, taking advantage of him this way, she wondered with a horrified shock. She was nearly about to take back her consent. Then he slowly smiled and leaned toward her, and every doubt scattered like leaves chased by a wild wind.

His face came closer and her eyes closed as his mouth met hers in a swift but possessive kiss. A kiss that set a seal upon her heart, affirming the promise they had made.

No, this wasn't a marriage based on love, Maura reflected. But despite her doubts, she'd go through with it. To set her life back on course. But more than that, for the sake of her child.

Three

———

Maura woke up at daybreak on Friday, well before the alarm. She had coffee, showered and carefully dressed in a brand-new pale-pink suit. The straight, knee-length skirt with a back slit made her slim legs look even longer, and the jacket's peplum style accentuated her small waist.

She removed from a small velvet box pearl earrings and a pearl choker, remembrances of her mother, and carefully put them on. It was times like this that Maura suddenly missed her family, especially her mother. She hadn't told anyone in Chicago about her decision to marry Doug, not even her sister or close friend, Liza.

She had always imagined a real church wedding, surrounded by friends and family, with a long, white gown and all the trimmings. But here she was, hurrying off to city hall to get married in secret—to a man she barely knew.

It had been just two days since Doug's impulsive proposal—and her impulsive acceptance. The time had passed in a dreamy haze as she and Doug had made their private plans. She had walked around the hospital, knowing she appeared perfectly normal on the outside, while inside she'd felt strangely unreal. She had agreed with Doug that a no-frills ceremony would be best, and through his step-brother, Seth Connelly, he'd found a judge who would marry them in his private chambers.

Doug had wanted to tell everyone right away about their plans to marry, but Maura had persuaded him to wait until it was a done deal. Maura had secretly worried that Doug might have had second thoughts—not that she would have blamed him. Or that maybe *she* would back out of the agreement. She'd known she wouldn't have been able to stand the embarrassment if she'd told people ahead of time and it hadn't worked out. She also hadn't wanted her co-workers asking a million questions or even giving her the usual, staff bridal shower. She'd felt like a bit of a fraud, knowing she wouldn't have been able to stand up to such close scrutiny.

Their hasty plans had given Doug only two days to clear his busy calendar and had given Maura little time to make room for Doug's belongings. She'd never seen his apartment, but had imagined the sparsely furnished studio, which reportedly didn't even have a real kitchen. Especially with the baby coming, her two-bedroom apartment was the logical choice as their new home.

Maura had distracted herself from her doubts by vigorously cleaning out her closets and the small second bedroom she used as a guest room and study. As she'd vacuumed and dusted, her gaze had kept returning to the blue sofa bed.

Would Doug be sleeping there at night...or sharing her bed? In the last two days they had talked over many practical matters regarding their marriage and quickly found agreement on every issue. But each time she'd considered bringing up sleeping arrangements, she'd shied away from the question. She'd felt so confused about it.

She was undeniably attracted to him.

If that kiss he'd given her prior to his proposal was any indication, he was attracted to her, as well. He had kissed her a few times since, in full view of their colleagues, too. When she'd asked him about it, he explained that he'd thought it was best to spark some gossip, so news of their marriage wouldn't come as a complete surprise. Then he'd jokingly added that they'd soon be married and she ought to get used it.

Maura knew she would have a part to play when they were out in public. They had agreed to act as if their marriage was a true love match, deciding it would make things so much easier at work and with both of their families, especially Doug's. Still, did that mean he expected their union to be a real one in every sense? Maura knew in her heart that if he wanted to make love to her, she wouldn't have the will to resist. But was that the best course for her to follow?

Their marriage still seemed so improbable at times, she often feared it would all dissolve in the blink of an eye, like a lovely but strange dream. Doug kept promising her everything would work out. But what if didn't?

But Maura tried to focus on the very immediate and positive present. She was running late, and Doug would be worried. She slipped a lipstick in her small handbag, then stepped into the impossibly high heels an eager salesgirl had talked her into. They matched the suit perfectly but were no match for Maura, who typically wore sturdy rubber-soled walking shoes for work every day. She wobbled more than a little in the heels, crossing the room to reach her dressing table. But as she approached the full-length mirror, she had to admit she looked…well, pretty darned good.

She placed the small matching hat on her head, secured it with pins and then pulled the pale-pink veil down over her face. It was just the feminine, glamorous touch she'd wanted. Maura felt as elegant and stylish as she'd ever been in her life.

She'd never been one to fuss over her appearance. But today was not only important because it was her wedding day, but because she finally had a chance to impress Doug. The only time he'd seen her dressed in anything but her baggy polyester uniform was the other night, when she'd been wearing her bathrobe and no makeup.

Maybe it was childish, but she knew he'd proposed mainly out of sympathy and because he was so noble. But when they met this morning she wanted to look so great that he wouldn't even recognize her. When they stood together and said their vows, she wanted him to feel anything but sympathy. She wanted him to be proud of her and feel he had no regrets in carrying through on his promise.

* * *

Doug paced anxiously in the old courthouse's cool marble lobby. He checked his watch for what seemed like the hundredth time, then pushed through a heavy door to stand outside. He took a deep breath of fresh air. It was a perfect morning in May, cloudless and mild, especially fair for Chicago. A perfect morning to get married. Friday appeared to be a big day in the matrimony department. A long line of couples had already assembled in the office on the fifth floor.

But his bride-to-be was late. Very late.

It wasn't like Maura. She was always so organized and punctual. He'd called her apartment twice, but there had been no answer. He knew that meant she must have left and was probably stuck in traffic. But it could also mean she was standing him up, he thought worriedly.

How many times in the past few days had she questioned their decision to marry? How many times had he needed to reassure her? But he knew it was right. Not logical perhaps. But simply and totally the right thing to do. For her and for him, as well.

He felt it in his bones, in his blood. He'd never felt so sure of anything before in his life. It was going to be easy to pretend that he and Maura were marrying for love because he felt so settled and sure about his decision. More settled even than the first time, when he had married Karen North, believing that he had made a lifelong commitment.

Karen was a golden girl, a tall, slim, gorgeous blonde. Every guy on campus wanted to get close to her. That was how Karen liked it, too. When they'd met, he'd never imagined she could go for a guy like him. For one thing, he was too serious, a real bore compared to Karen, either working one of his part-time jobs or in the library, trying to keep up his grades for the scholarship putting him through undergraduate studies and the one he wanted for med school. Besides, he was pathetically poor compared to her family.

But maybe that was what attracted Karen to him in the first place. He was certainly different from the people she'd known her entire life, growing up in her affluent Lake Forest cocoon. She'd admired him at first, found him so dedicated and with such strong values. But her admiration soon grew thin, Doug reflected. Once they were married, during his first year of medical school, Karen realized that unlike many young doctors, he was not dedicated to the idea of making money.

This came as a great shock to his young wife. She was sure that sooner or later, if she cajoled, teased and pressured him enough, Doug would come around. But her tactics pushed them even further apart. To the breaking point. By the time she announced that she'd found someone else—a plastic surgeon who shared her values, not surprisingly—there was nothing much left of their marriage to mourn, Doug reflected. Only the fact that they'd never had children.

Well, best not to dwell on the past. Not this morning, of all days. He hardly thought of Karen anymore. It still hurt if he allowed his thoughts to drift there. The betrayal. The humiliation. He had found it hard to allow anyone close again. All his relationships since that time had either totally bored him or had gone down in flames. He just couldn't seem to connect or give a woman what she wanted emotionally.

But Maura was different. He'd felt so from the first. She was sweet and openhearted, totally sincere. They shared the same values, the same outlook, the same dedication to their work. At times Doug felt so attuned to her, it was simply uncanny. Maura was the complete opposite of his ex-wife, that was for sure.

But did he love her? He respected her, admired her, felt protective of her and certainly had deep feelings for her. Feelings that even he hadn't been aware of until the other night. He knew now he'd been secretly jealous of her relationship with Scott Walker. He'd felt pleased when he'd heard that they'd broken up, although he hadn't admitted that.

But did he love her? Ultimately, the answer was no, he did not.

But Doug was equally certain he would never fall in love with any woman again. Not the way he had fallen so head over heels with Karen, as if she owned him, heart and soul. He never wanted to feel that way again about anybody.

He did want a child. And in the past few days he wondered if it was dishonest of him to offer Maura marriage but never explain that part of his reason. But each time he had the urge to tell her, some intuition warned him to hold back until they were married. He just had the feeling she wouldn't understand and might even back out of their plan.

And he didn't want that. He wanted to help her and help himself.

Some might consider what he felt for Maura a slim foundation for a step as weighty as marriage, but he knew it was solid and real. A bedrock to build a life on. Not some airy-fairy romantic fantasy or sexual chemistry that ignites in a flash, then burns out just as swiftly.

They would have an equal partnership. They would make a life together and raise Maura's child.

While he loved taking care of other people's children, healing them and making them strong and happy again, his professional satisfaction would never take the place of raising children of his own. It was an issue he and Karen had talked about often—argued about often, too.

But by the time they were financially ready to start a family, the relationship was already on the ropes. Karen knew how much he wanted a baby and had used that to blackmail him, refusing to get pregnant or even to make love, unless he gave in to her demands.

She wanted him to stop taking on poor patients who couldn't pay, she wanted him to leave Chicago General and start a practice in an upper-class community where he'd have regular hours and make more money. That was the price he had to pay to have a baby with her. She believed she held the winning hand. But her tactics pushed him even further away. As much as he'd wanted a child, he wouldn't "pay" for one by denying his true values and motivation for becoming a doctor. Besides, his speciality in pediatric cardiology made regular hours impossible. But Karen didn't seem to understand that. Or didn't want to. She kept insisting he would give up that part of his practice and just work as a general pediatrician. But Doug felt that request, too, was extremely unfair of her.

More important, he knew it was wrong to bring a child into their troubled relationship.

Now fate had brought him both a wife and a child. Doug sometimes wondered at his own impulsive decision to show up at Maura's door and propose marriage. But now it seemed as if he'd been handed a chance to make things right for Maura. And for himself. He pushed aside his doubts and grasped that chance with both hands. Now if only his reluctant bride would appear and they could get the nerve-wracking part of this entire business over with. He knew everything after that would work out just fine.

Doug spotted a taxi pull over to the curb and a woman start to emerge. God, what a woman, he thought as he watched her stand upright and smooth out her skirt before taking on the long flight of granite steps.

Was it Maura, he wondered. He thought he recognized her fine profile, her tall, slim build, but he couldn't see her hair, pinned up under a provocative little hat. And he couldn't see her face, with her chin dipped down as she climbed the steps and much of her face covered by a veil.

He suddenly realized he'd never seen Maura dressed up. Never seen her in anything but her uniform, actually. The woman approaching him could be Maura. He allowed himself to take a longer, more appraising look, then couldn't quite draw his gaze away. She was simply gorgeous. A total knockout. From her softly veiled features to her sexy high heels.

He felt disloyal watching this way if she didn't turn out to be his intended. But Doug couldn't quite take his eyes off this alluring vision, her perfect figure artfully displayed in a stylish, tailored suit, a petal-pink confection. All you could see of her face was a pouting pink mouth, her lips tempting to be tasted, explored, savored.

As she walked purposefully up the steps, straight toward him, his mouth grew dry. He still wasn't sure if it was Maura, his bride-to-be, and felt a mixture of lustful excitement and guilt watching the mystery woman's lean shapely legs carry her the remaining steps to where he stood.

No crime in looking, he wryly reflected. Married or not, I'm only a man. And this woman makes me glad of it, he laughed to himself.

Then she stood before him, inches away, her back to the early-morning sun, her face still shadowed by the veil.

"Waiting for me?" she asked in a breathless voice.

"Well, I...I—" Doug stammered and for the life of him, he couldn't tell for absolute sure it was Maura.

Then she laughed and lifted her chin so he could see her face. Maura's face, familiar, yet somehow exciting, unknown territory. Her smile lit up her lovely features, making her beautiful green eyes shine with emotion. He'd never noticed that before and he knew he'd be a lucky man to look up each morning and find that smile shining just for him.

Doug glanced down, suddenly remembering the bouquet of flowers in his hand, cream-colored roses, pink phlox and miniature orchids. The colors matched her outfit perfectly, as if it had been planned.

"These are for you," he said.

"What beautiful flowers. Thank you."

"You're very welcome." He knew he was still staring, but couldn't help himself. Her expression of delight and the fresh flowers in her grasp emphasized her natural beauty even more.

"Sorry I was late. My taxi was caught in traffic."

"I thought as much," he replied smoothly, though he'd actually considered the worst.

"You didn't recognize me at first, did you?" Her eyes sparkled with a teasing light.

He shrugged. "Of course I did."

"Oh? Why didn't you say something? You were staring at me as if I was a total stranger."

Doug paused for just a heartbeat. Then he leaned closer, slipping his arm around her waist in a tight, possessive gesture that made Maura's stomach drop to her toes.

"I was staring at you because you look so beautiful you take my breath away," he admitted in a harsh whisper. He dropped a hard kiss on her mouth, then quickly pulled his head away.

"Now let's get married, Maura. I think you've kept me waiting long enough."

When he pulled back a bit, Maura stared up at him, too astounded by his words and gesture to speak. Maura took the arm he offered, and with a deep breath, walked into city hall at his side.

The ceremony was brief and to the point, as Maura had expected. As the judge read the official script from a small black book, Maura could hardly concentrate on the words. She suddenly noticed how wonderful Doug looked, how tall and fit he appeared in his dark-blue suit, stark white shirt and burgundy silk tie. His brown hair was combed back and looked newly cut, his lean cheeks smoothly shaved. She could hardly recall seeing a man more handsome, and it was hard to believe he would very soon and very officially be her husband.

The clerk asked for the rings, and Doug produced two gold bands. Her ring was inlaid with three small rubies and engraved with a vine-like design. Doug's was quite plain and masculine looking, she noticed as she slipped it on his finger. She had forgotten all about rings and stared down at hers in surprise as the clerk finished the ceremony.

Once pronounced husband and wife, Doug's kiss to seal their vows was tantalizingly brief. Immediately after, in the split second they moved apart, she glimpsed a questioning look in his eyes and something more, a look that was pure male desire and sent a chill down to her toes.

Then, just as quickly, that look vanished, his expression showing little emotion at all. The clerk asked them to sign some papers. As Maura smiled and stood beside her handsome groom, the reality of what she'd done began to sink in.

She felt practically light-headed as they left the dark building and stepped out into the sunshine. But Doug seemed unfazed and clearly had plans. He took her hand as they walked down the stone steps—either as a gesture of affection or merely because he noticed her wobbling on her perilously high heels.

They started walking toward his car, and Doug kept firm hold of her hand. People were glancing at them, some smiled and said, ''Good luck.'' Maura remembered her bouquet and realized it was a dead give-away—everyone knew they were newly married.

"I've made reservations for lunch at Bistro 53, but we don't have to go there if you'd rather not," Doug said, mentioning the city's latest epicurean sensation. "Have you tried it yet?"

"No problem," Maura laughed. "I really don't keep up with the hot spots much."

"I thought maybe Scott had taken you there. He liked to try all the latest places."

"We went out often enough, I guess. But after a while, mostly I cooked in. It was so much...cozier."

She didn't mean to mar their fine morning with bitterness, but she could hardly help herself when she talked about Scott.

Doug glanced at her, his mouth turned down in a frown. He abruptly stopped in his tracks, and she had to grip his arm to keep from stumbling. He didn't seem to notice.

"Listen, let's make a pact. From now on, unless absolutely necessary, no mention of Scott. We're starting off here with a clean slate. Agreed?"

"Agreed." Maura nodded and smiled. Doug was right. And so perceptive. Memories of Scott only brought her down. Her relationship with Doug was going to be difficult enough without lugging along that heavy baggage.

"On to Bistro 53," she said brightly. "What a nice surprise."

"It's our wedding day, Maura. We need to celebrate," Doug replied with an indulgent smile.

They reached his car and Doug opened the door for her. She'd been in the black sports car once before, but didn't recall that it was quite so small and so low. Her narrow skirt made it hard to wriggle into her seat.

She sensed Doug looking hungrily at a length of leg, revealed by the skirt's slit, then quickly glancing away. Well, they were married. The man was entitled to check out what he'd gotten for his trouble, she thought wryly.

Doug maneuvered the sports car easily through the city's heavy traffic, and they were soon driving on picturesque Lake Shore Drive, headed for the city's most fashionable neighborhood. At the restaurant a valet parked the car and the maître d' led them to a secluded table by the window, the magnificent lake in full view.

Perhaps it was their newlywed status, or maybe Doug had surreptitiously tipped the entire staff. Maura was not sure of the reason, but couldn't help notice that they were treated royally. Even better than one would expect in such an elegant restaurant. The decor was gorgeous, the food sublime. Maura's wedding day jitters soon dissolved, and she once again felt her familiar, warm rapport with Doug.

"What treatment," Maura finally remarked when their waiter brought them yet another special dish, compliments of the chef—an hors d'oeuvre portion of lobster Napoleon, with a delicate sherry sauce.

"You must come here often to rate such attention," she finally said.

Doug took a moment to swallow a small bite of his lobster, savoring the flavor. "Hmm, that was good. But no, they don't really know me. I've only come here once before, for lunch with my father. But I suppose the Connelly name goes far in this city. And it's your name now, too, Maura,'' he added with a small smile.

''The Connelly name. Oh, of course,'' she replied, feeling foolish for overlooking the fact that Doug was part of that eminent Chicago family.

The name brought to mind privilege, power, celebrity and of course fabulous wealth. None of which she associated with Doug. But shortly after they'd met, she'd heard bits and pieces of how he'd recently discovered he was a member of the prestigious clan. She had never asked Doug directly about the story but had always been curious.

She suddenly worried that perhaps Doug suspected her motives for agreeing to their marriage. Maybe he thought she'd only married him for his newfound wealth and connections. But then she swept the thought aside. Doug knew very well she would never resort to such a tactic. Not even to protect her child. During the past few days he'd had plenty of time to present her with a prenuptial agreement, to protect his interests should they divorce, and had never once even mentioned it. It made her feel good to realize how much he truly trusted her.

''Tell me, Doug. How did you first find out that you were a Connelly?'' Maura asked. ''When we first met, your last name was Barnett, right?''

''Yes, that's right. It was important to Grant Connelly, my father, that my brother and I change our names to his, once we discovered our true relationship. My brother was more resistant to it than I. But I'm getting ahead of myself,'' he added. He paused and sat back in his chair. ''Well, let's see… I've already told you that I was raised by my mother, Hannah. It was just me and my twin brother, Chance.''

Maura already knew that Doug had a twin brother and had a close relationship with him. Chance was a Navy SEAL and had recently gotten engaged to be married, she recalled.

''Naturally, as we got older we were curious about our father and asked my mom a lot of questions,'' Doug continued. ''But she would never tell us anything. Just that she was quite young when she'd known him and had loved him. But they couldn't be together and they were never in touch. I guess I got the idea that she didn't even know how to find this mystery man even if she wanted to,'' Doug added, shaking his head. ''Little did I realize his picture was in the financial section or the society pages of the newspaper almost every day.

''She'd never say anything negative about our father, either,'' Doug continued. ''In fact, she gave us the impression he was a good man. A decent person. But as I got older, I just couldn't buy it anymore. In a way, I guess I came to hate my father without even knowing him,'' Doug confessed, ''this faceless, heartless guy who had abandoned my poor mother when she needed him most. He didn't seem very nice or decent to me,'' Doug said bitterly. ''Still, my mother protected him. Her loyalty was limitless. And absolutely undeserved by my father, I thought.''

''It must have been very hard for you, dealing with all those feelings growing up.''

''Yes, it was.'' He met her gaze directly and for a moment she saw what he must have been like as a small boy, brooding over questions about his father and feelings of love and protection for his mother. He glanced out at the lake and took a sip of his coffee.

"When my mother died, one of her last words was my father's name. My brother and I knew instinctively that she had finally told us the identity of our father. But by then we weren't nearly so intent on finding him and confronting him. And we also wondered if it was true. My mother was heavily medicated in her final days. We wondered if she had been rational."

"Yes, I see," Maura replied, considering Doug's story.

"But as I went through her belongings, I found her diary. I'll never be sure if that was her intention all along, or if in her illness she'd merely neglected to destroy it. She'd recorded the entire story, her attraction and romance to an older man when she was just a student and working as a waitress in a diner near the campus. The man was young, ambitious and clearly headed for great things. She'd been his lover, confidante and everything in between. My mother believed in him totally. She was not only beautiful and intelligent, but a very loving person. So how could he resist her? According to her diary, he had claimed to love her, too. Though he must have seen that their age difference and different situations in life made any long-lasting ties unlikely." Doug looked out at the lake for a moment, and she could tell from his expression that it was hard for him to tell this story.

"Then, while her lover was traveling abroad, he met another woman. A woman more suited to his ambitions and plans. My mother read about their romance in the society column. This woman was a world figure—a princess, in fact, of marriageable age, so if she so much as smiled at a man it made all the celebrity gossip columns.''

Emma Connelly had been a princess of some small country, Maura recalled. The place was called Altaria, wasn't it? And Emma had given up her royal life to marry Grant Connelly, who was then just an up-and-coming American businessman.

''My mother, a waitress and part-time student, knew she could never compete with this rival,'' Doug continued. ''She also believed that my father would be far happier with his new love. So she made a truly self-sacrificing choice and simply disappeared from his life, without him ever knowing why. Or ever knowing that she was pregnant with his sons. He never knew what had happened to her or why she'd gone.''

''What a story,'' Maura said, awestruck. ''She must have loved him very much.''

Doug glanced at her, a look of surprise in his amber eyes.

''Yes, she did. Enough to put her own needs aside, even the needs of her children, in order to spare him the dilemma of making him choose. But it took me a while to realize that. While it only took you about five seconds,'' he added with a small smile.

Maura smiled and looked at the lake. ''Women usually have a better understanding of these things than men.''

''Men are a bit dense,'' Doug offered. ''Anyway, the truth was, my father never knew about my brother and me. This faceless mystery man I had hated all my life wasn't the heartless monster I'd imagined at all.''

''And he turned out to be Grant Connelly,'' Maura said quietly.

''Yes, the famous Grant Connelly. I couldn't believe it at first. But all the facts added up—the times, the dates, the places. My brother and I couldn't decide if we wanted to confront our father. Or how to do it. We thought maybe he'd deny our claim and think we were fortune hunters.''

''I never thought of that, but I suppose wealthy families like the Connellys have that problem all the time, people claiming they're related and due some piece of the family wealth,'' Maura said.

''Exactly,'' Doug replied. ''But at the same time I was discovering these secrets, an investigative reporter working on a story about my father had dug up the information and told him he'd had two sons by Hannah Barnett. So we ended up meeting soon after that. When I finally confronted my father, he verified everything. I do believe he loved my mother and was terribly sorry she'd never asked him for help. That alone meant a lot to me,'' Doug said in a tone edged with emotion. ''It went a long way toward changing my feelings about him and changing my anger to forgiveness.''

Maura didn't know what to say. The story was remarkable and a deeply personal confession. She felt so much for Doug, so much for the troubles he'd endured. She could see that, as much as he'd wanted to tell her about this important moment in his life, telling had been hard for him.

She reached across the table and took hold of his hand. "It was good of you to forgive him," she said.

"It wasn't nearly as hard as I'd imagined it would be," Doug reflected with a thoughtful expression. "My father is a remarkable man. He's done everything in his power to show us how much he regrets not having been there while we were growing up. The entire family has been wonderful to me and Chance. I have eight new stepsiblings and have met all of them so far, except for the oldest, Daniel, who is in Altaria and will soon be crowned king."

Wow was the only word that came to Maura's mind.

"I can hardly wait for you to meet Grant and Emma," he added.

"I'm looking forward to it," Maura replied diplomatically.

"I know you pretty well now, Maura. You look as if I'd just invited you to go bungee jumping off the Sears Tower." Doug's laugh was quiet and deep. "Don't worry. It will be fine." He twined his long lean fingers together with hers. "They'll love you, I'm sure of it. Don't be surprised if they throw us a big party."

The idea of being the center of attraction at a celebration hosted by the famous Grant and Emma Connelly was even more intimidating. Maura struggled to hide her alarm.

"You won't tell them that I'm pregnant, will you?" she asked suddenly.

He met her gaze, still holding her hand. "Not if you don't want me to."

"I don't. I mean, they'll find out fairly soon, no

matter what. As will everyone at the hospital,'' she added. ''But for now I'd prefer if we kept it to ourselves. Everyone is going to think you made me pregnant and then had to marry me,'' she added. Then another thought occurred to her, which was even more upsetting. ''They'll also think I was seeing you and Scott at the same time.''

''Who cares what anyone thinks?'' Doug said, his expression serious and intense. He gently squeezed her hand. ''I know we've done the right thing. This is going to work out for us. Let's just take it one day at a time, okay?'' His gaze implored her, and Maura couldn't help but smile.

''Yes, you're right. This is my life and I shouldn't give a fig what anyone thinks.''

''That's my girl.'' His smile grew wider, his reply giving Maura a slight jolt. She was indeed his girl now. More than that, she was his wife. She looked down at their hands clasped together on the table and noticed her shiny new wedding band.

''I never thanked you for the ring,'' she said. ''It's really beautiful.''

He turned her hand to see the stone better. Maura looked at it, too. The jewel sparkled in its golden setting, looking even lovelier than when he'd slipped it on her finger.

''Since we bypassed the engagement stage I wanted to get you something more than a plain gold band. Are you sure you like it? You don't have to say so just to be polite.''

Maura was touched—and even surprised—by his desire to please her. ''It's exactly what I would have chosen. It's perfect, Doug. Really.''

"Good. I'm glad." His gaze met hers again. His smile grew wider—even white teeth against tanned skin. Deep dimples appeared in his lean cheeks, tiny lines fanned out at the corners of his eyes. He was really so attractive. It just about took her breath away. Maura couldn't hold his gaze any longer and glanced away.

Doug paid the check, and they left their table. As they stood at the restaurant door, waiting for the valet to bring Doug's car, his cell phone rang. "My office," he said to Maura as he answered it.

Maura nodded. She knew Doug had arranged for another doctor to cover his patients today, and his office wouldn't be calling unless it was an emergency. At least she had a true understanding of his job. Marrying a doctor was not her ideal, but she knew the demands of his job would never be an issue for her. The grueling hours and priority of patients over family had destroyed many marriages. Maybe that was what had happened in Doug's first marriage, Maura thought.

Doug clicked off the phone and turned to Maura, his expression a mixture of regret and urgency. "I'm needed at the hospital. The Harris boy is in trouble. The doctor covering for me has another emergency and the attending is swamped."

"Don't worry, I understand," Maura assured him. "Good, here's the car," she added as the valet delivered Doug's sports car. "You'd better go. I'll get a cab."

"Are you sure? I could drop you off. It's not that far out of the way."

"I'll be fine. Why waste all that time?"

Doug started to go, then paused and stared deeply into her eyes. "I'm so sorry. I hate to run off on you like this. Especially today."

The tender look in his eyes touched her. She smiled at him and then, without thinking, touched his cheek with her hand.

"Don't be silly. I understand."

Besides, it's not like it's a real wedding day. Or a real marriage, she thought to add. Yet, something stopped her. At that brief moment she felt truly married to him.

She was quickly distracted by the stunning look of gratitude and relief on his handsome face. He swiftly bent toward her and dropped a quick, hard kiss on her mouth.

"I'll make it up to you later. Promise," he added as he got into his car. "And don't worry about unpacking my stuff. I'll take care of it."

"Don't worry," Maura said as she stepped back on the curb.

Maura watched the car quickly pull away. The hospital was not very far. He'd be there soon, she was sure. As for herself, she'd change into comfortable clothes and start unpacking Doug's things, no matter what he said. What else did she have to do on her wedding day?

Grant Connelly entered the spacious family room and settled on a large sofa across from his wife. She looked up from her book and briefly smiled at him. Their schedules were both so busy they rarely had time to have dinner together or spend an evening like this, simply relaxing in each other's company.

Grant was relishing the downtime. He casually studied the financial news of the day as Emma focused on her thick historical novel. Emma loved history. She had so many interests and still, after all these years, had so much intellectual curiosity and a drive to learn new things. That was something Grant had always admired about her.

Emma put her book aside and looked over at him.

"I'm worried about Seth," she said. "What if it doesn't go well?"

Grant met his wife's concerned gaze. After twenty years their son Seth was meeting with his birth mother, Angie Donahue. If all had gone according to plans, at this very moment, they would be sitting down to dinner and getting to know each other again.

Seth had not seen Angie since he was twelve years old, and Angie had basically given up on him. Seth had arrived at the Connelly home angry, sad and confused—doing poorly at school and a party to some minor brushes with the law. If not for our understanding and love, who knows what would have happened to him, Grant reflected.

But he was fine. More than fine, he was happy, successful, and productive. A man Grant was proud to call his son.

"I understand why you're worried, Emma. Really, I do," Grant assured his wife. "But it's only natural that Seth would be curious about his mother. You have to remember he's a grown man. She can't hurt him anymore."

"I worry for no reason, I guess," Emma conceded. "But I can't help remembering the way Seth was when he came to us, so angry and confused. So…damaged by her.''

"I remember," Grant agreed. "But that was long ago.''

Grant sighed, recalling Seth's first days in the Connelly household. Seth was mad at the world and wanted to punish every adult in it—particularly Grant—for his confusion and unhappiness. But day by day, with patience and understanding on the part of his new family, he gradually came to trust, respect and even love Grant, Emma and his stepsiblings. Military school helped, as well, to discipline Seth's strong spirit, strengthen his character and sharpen his fine mind.

"It was a difficult time for all of us, but we got through it.''

"Yes, we did," Emma met his gaze and smiled, communicating volumes in a single look, as only long-married couples can do.

It had been a dark moment in their marriage when Grant admitted that Angie Donahue had given birth to his son and that he'd been secretly supporting his former secretary and the boy for over twelve years.

Emma had been crushed by the betrayal, and they had even separated for a time. But when they'd finally reconciled, his wife, with her gloriously generous heart, had even agreed to take Seth and raise him as one of her own.

Grant had the sudden urge to thank his wife again for pulling them through, for being so forgiving toward him, so accepting of his mistakes and flaws. But words could never communicate the depth of those feelings. He simply tried to show her every day how grateful he was to still be married to her.

"He'll be all right, Emma. You'll see. He's always had questions about Angie and that part of his life. Questions we couldn't answer for him," Grant reflected. "Maybe filling in the pieces will help him sort out some issues in his own life."

"Yes, I think you're right. He's done so well for himself," she said proudly. "But I know he still has to work out some issues about his childhood. And about Angie. Maybe that's what's been holding him back from meeting some nice girl and getting married," she added.

Grant laughed. "Seth is never lacking for female companionship, as far as I can see."

His son's striking good looks, success as an attorney and powerful personality made him a magnet for feminine attention. Seth's problem was quite the opposite, Grant thought, more a case of having too many choices.

"I'm not talking about running around," Emma said. "I'm talking about falling in love. Settling down. These girls he brings home are gorgeous. But none of them seems to keep his interest for very long. I just want to see him happy, with someone he can really love. That's all."

"That's what we want for all our children, isn't it?" Grant asked his wife. "If they could each find half the happiness and love I've found with you, dear, they'd be very lucky indeed."

Emma stared at him a moment, a loving look in her sparkling eyes. "I feel the same about you, too. You know that," she said quietly. Then, in a different tone, "But enough. You'll make me get all weepy and I'm trying to finish this book."

Emma opened her book again with determination, though he could tell she wasn't really reading it.

"If you say so," Grant replied with a laugh.

He still loved her so much he felt his heart swell. It didn't seem possible that a man could live with a woman for so long and still have these feelings. He'd honestly meant what he'd said about their children. He truly wished that each of their sons and daughters could find the kind of marriage he and Emma shared. No amount of worldly fame or even material success could match that priceless treasure.

Coincidentally, Grant was still pondering these thoughts when the housekeeper announced a call from his son Doug. Grant picked up the call immediately.

"Doug, how good to hear from you. What's new?"

Emma put down her book. "Tell him I said hello," she whispered.

Then she was silenced by the amazed expression on Grant's face.

"You're kidding," Grant exclaimed. "That's fantastic news. Hold on. I have to tell Emma. She won't believe it."

"What's happened? Is he okay?" Emma asked in a rush.

"Doug got married today to a nurse he works with at the hospital. Her name is Maura."

"Married?" Emma clutched her chest. She felt breathless. "I can't believe it. Here, let me talk," she insisted, holding her hand out for the phone.

Grant sat back as his wife ecstatically offered her congratulations and then proceeded to interrogate

Doug about his new wife. Well, he deserved a little of that for eloping on them, Grant thought. Not that Emma would let him get off without some type of family celebration. He could already hear her firming up plans for Doug to bring his new wife over for brunch on Sunday.

She handed the phone back to Grant, and he added a few more congratulatory words to his son. Then Doug had to run. He was calling from the hospital and was needed again on the floor.

When Grant turned to Emma, she literally clapped her hands together. "I'd never imagined Doug to be the type to elope. It's so romantic. I can't wait to meet his wife. She must be terrific."

"Well, at least we got one son married off tonight, dear," Grant said dryly. "Not bad work for one evening."

Emma ignored his remark. "We'll have to give them a party, of course. Something informal but nice. Where she can meet the whole family."

Grant recognized that look in his wife's eye. She was off and running, as he had predicted. There was no stopping her now.

"I'd like to have something outdoors. Maybe at the lake house," Emma continued, mentioning their sprawling country retreat on Lake Geneva.

"Sounds perfect to me, but we'd better wait to ask Doug and his new bride what they think, before you call up the caterers and send out invitations," he teased her.

"They're coming for brunch next weekend," Emma said. "I can't wait to meet her. I didn't even know he was seeing anyone."

"Sounds like a whirlwind romance. Doug strikes me as the type who makes up his mind about something and does it."

"Well, that's the way it is sometimes. You meet someone and you just know," Emma replied.

"Yes, that's very true." Grant remembered the first time he set eyes on Emma. Everyone else in the world seemed to just disappear. Within moments of saying hello, he knew she was the one. The complications of her life—and his—didn't matter. He knew he had to have her.

"Here, give me the phone," Emma said urgently. "This is big news. I have a lot of calls to make."

Grant laughed and handed his wife the phone. The secret was out. By the time Doug woke up tomorrow, the entire Connelly clan would know he was married.

Four

$\mathbf{M}$aura heard the key scraping in the lock and then the sound of the door opening and closing again as Doug let himself in. The glowing numbers on the bedside table clock read 2:32 a.m. He'd been called back to the hospital on an emergency hours ago, just as Maura was coming in after her work shift. They'd barely had the chance to exchange two words with each other before Doug had disappeared again.

That was the way their lives had been for the past week, like two people chasing each other in a revolving door. When friends at work asked how she was enjoying married life, she honestly couldn't say. She hardly felt married at all. Except for the scant evidence of her husband's existence—a shirt slung over the back of a chair, the lingering scent of aftershave in the bathroom—she hardly felt as if anyone at all was sharing her apartment.

He was trying to be quiet and considerate, but she had always been a light sleeper. The hot, muggy weather tonight made sleep even harder. She didn't have any air-conditioning, and the small window fan didn't help much.

She could picture Doug's face as clearly as if he were standing right next to her, his tired expression and five-o'clock shadow. He would be in the mood to talk over his case, especially if there had been some difficult treatment decisions to make. Ironically, they had talked much more in the hospital when they were merely friends than they had so far as husband and wife.

Should she get up and go to him? See how his emergency turned out? Then she rejected the idea, just as she had so many other nights. What would he think, seeing her at his bedroom door in the middle of the night? He would assume she wanted something more than conversation, that was for sure.

What did she want?

Maura honestly didn't know.

When he had moved his things into her apartment, just before their wedding day, Maura had put most of his belongings in her spare bedroom. It seemed the logical place to store the many boxes until they had time to sort things out. She had not purposely intended to send Doug a message that she expected him to sleep there. But she had been asleep by the time he'd gotten home their wedding night, and the next morning, she found him there.

The next day, and all the days since, she never had the courage to talk about it. After all, he didn't seem to mind sleeping alone. He seemed to assume that would be the arrangement. If he'd expected something different, wouldn't he have made it clear by now?

Maybe, despite the tantalizing way he'd kissed her now and again, he wasn't all that attracted to her, she thought. Though she had to admit, at least to herself, that she felt different about him. Much different.

So that was why she felt awkward going to him now, dressed in her nightgown. That was why she felt their relationship tense and strained during those rare moments they'd been alone together here since they married.

If this was the kind of tension she had to face for the rest of her life, Maura didn't think she could stand it.

When she was sure he had gone into his room and closed the door, Maura got up and headed for the kitchen. She couldn't sleep without a cold drink. She really wanted ice tea...but milk would be better for the baby. Cookies and milk, maybe. No, just the milk, she revised as she stared into the fridge. She didn't want to gain too much weight. But one cookie couldn't hurt. Would it?

Lost in her calorie quandary, Maura didn't notice Doug's tall, powerful form in the doorway.

"If it isn't my phantom wife," he greeted her.

"Doug." Startled, she turned to him. "I thought you were asleep."

"I thought the same about you."

His words were simple, but in his gruff, low tone she heard something more. She met his heavy-lidded gaze, then pulled out the milk carton, making a conscious effort to keep it from slipping right through her shaky hands.

He was bare-chested and barefoot, wearing just a pair of faded jeans that hung low on his lean hips. She'd never seen him with so little clothes on, and Maura could barely keep her eyes off his body.

The flash of pure hunger in his gaze made her suddenly self-conscious. She was wearing only a short nightgown, the sheerest one she owned, due to the steamy weather. She quickly sat down at the kitchen table, thankful that there was only a small circle of light cast by the fixture over the sink.

"Sorry if I made too much noise when I came in. I was trying to be quiet."

"It wasn't you. I couldn't sleep that well. It's so hot tonight." She busied herself pouring the milk, carefully avoiding his smoldering gaze.

"Yes, it is," he agreed. "Too hot for May."

And getting hotter by the second in here, she nearly replied.

"I heard we're in for some rain. Maybe that will cool things off," he said.

"Maybe," she agreed.

Here they were alone in the dark, both of them barely dressed, and all he could do was talk about the weather. Now, if that didn't prove he didn't mind sleeping alone in the spare room, Maura asked herself, what did?

He leaned back against the counter, watching her. She felt her mouth grow dry as he crossed his arms over his chest, his wide shoulders and upper arms bunching up into impressive knots of muscle. Thick swirls of soft brown hair emphasized his muscular chest. Her fingers itched to test its texture. Her gaze moved lower, to the flat stretch of abdomen above the edge of his jeans and a thin line of dark hair that disappeared into his waistband. She forced herself to look away and think of something else. Something other than Doug's amazing body…

"How's your patient?" she asked suddenly.

"A very good prognosis. She'll probably leave the hospital by the end of the week."

"That's great," Maura replied, her thought distracted by his alluring image, her fingertips imagining the smoothness of his tanned skin, or the rough stubble on his chin.

"Maura…I'm afraid I haven't been a very good husband to you." Doug's deep, halting tone cut into her wandering fantasies.

"Don't be silly. We haven't seen nearly enough of each other the past few days to tell what kind of husband you are," she replied in a joking tone. "Or for that matter, what kind of wife I'll be."

"You're a great cook," he pointed out. "I've been meaning to tell you. But you're never around when I'm eating the food you've left for me. Leaving a note seemed…silly," he admitted.

"I never find any leftovers. I figured you'd either politely hidden the stuff in the trash or you like my cooking. Or maybe you're hungry enough to eat anything."

"I like your cooking. Especially the beef stew. That was good." He smiled, a flash of even white teeth against bronzed skin, his expression sending even more heat shooting through her body than usual, it seemed. "It was good of you to fix me anything at all."

"It was nothing." She liked to do things for him. He'd been so kind to her, so generous. Yet she couldn't find the right words to explain her feelings. "What are wives for?" she joked.

"I'm sure you're beat at the end of the day. Especially being pregnant."

"I like to do it, honestly. It helps me unwind." Her voice lifted on a shaky note as he closed the small space between them and stood beside her chair.

"From work, you mean? Or are you worried about something else?"

She gazed up at him. He looked so big and powerful, looming over her in the shadowy light, his rugged features fixed in an intense expression. A look of concern, for sure. But beyond that, one of pure, masculine desire that made her pulse race. She turned and looked forward again, feeling frozen in place.

How could she begin to explain that it was him. Sharing this apartment with him, being married, but not quite knowing where they stood. Or how he felt about her.

And wanting him like crazy. Like right now, for instance.

"It's nothing in particular," she said softly.

"Go ahead, you can tell me," he urged her quietly. When she still didn't speak, he put his large, strong hand on her bare shoulder, moving it in small, sensuous circles that made every nerve ending in her body spring to life.

"I don't think this is going to work." She swallowed hard. "I still don't even understand why you married me. I'm not exactly the type that drives men crazy,'' she added, aiming for an ironic note that didn't sound self-pitying.

"No, you're definitely not," he agreed, his tone so deep, and definite, it made her heart sink. "But maybe I didn't want a woman who would drive me crazy. Maybe I've already done that."

"You know what I mean, Doug. You didn't need to settle for me. You could have had anyone."

She was totally and absolutely serious, voicing doubts she'd had from the start. Yet she heard Doug reply with a low, sexy laugh, as he moved to stand behind her, his other hand coming to rest on her empty shoulder.

"But I picked you." His head dipped down low, so that his mouth was right next to her ear before he spoke again. "Now you're stuck with me. Is that what's really worrying you, Maura?"

"No…not at all. Don't be silly," she said softly.

"Good, then." His words, spoken so deep and low, penetrated her very bones.

She felt an impulse to reply, but then the words were stolen from her lips as she felt his heavy warm hands brush back her long hair.

"Don't think so much, Maura. Don't doubt," he softly urged her. "I know this will work. Just give it some time."

The truth was at that moment she couldn't think. She could barely breathe as his touch glided over her smooth, bare skin. Maura felt her senses tingle with awareness, her ragged nerves instantly soothed yet charged with an energy that was totally electric.

"How's that?" Doug asked quietly.

"That's…good," she finally managed. "Very… good."

She hadn't even been aware of the hard knots in her neck and shoulders until Doug's strong fingers found them and slowly dissolved them with a touch that was pure magic.

"Your hair is so beautiful. You should wear it down like this more often."

Her eyes were closed, and his deep voice seemed to reach her from far away.

"It's not very practical that way for work," she finally replied.

"At home. With me, I mean." Doug's lips were close to her cheek, and she could feel his warm breath on her skin.

"Yes, with you," she replied softly, feeling as if she were talking in a dream.

She felt him kiss her nape, his mouth wet and hot. A bolt of molten heat flashed through her body. She knew that at that moment she would probably agree to anything he asked. A liquid languor flowed into her limbs, warming every inch of her body.

"Maura," he said softly. "I've missed you. I've missed talking with you like this."

She felt her heartbeat quicken. She'd missed him, too. And during those brief hours they'd spent alone here together, she'd felt such a disturbing tension, as if every movement, every breath, wound the sexual tension between them even higher.

"I…I missed you, too," she admitted softly, without even opening her eyes. His touch felt so good, almost hypnotic. Her senses were focused entirely on the feelings he had so easily aroused. His hands slid down from her shoulders to her arms, his fingertips just grazing the sides of her breasts. Her nipples tingled with awareness, instantly taut.

Her eyes were still closed and her head was tilted slightly to one side when she felt Doug's warm lips on the curve of her supple neck. His palms glided down the length of her arms, then up again as his soft, enticing kisses slowly followed the line of her shoulder. Maura felt her body shudder with excitement, every nerve ending tingling. She was shocked by her response, the warm pulse at her center, aching for Doug's touch. What had come over her? Her body had never been awakened so quickly by any man before.

When she felt Doug's hands reach around and cup her aching breasts, she heard herself release a long, deep sigh. She instinctively reached up and covered his hands with her own, urging him to explore her even further. She heard him sigh, exciting her even more as he stroked the hardened nipples, then slipped down the thin straps of nightgown. Maura felt herself sinking into a whirlpool of sensations and she sighed with satisfaction at his pleasuring caress.

Then suddenly he had moved around the chair and was crouched down next to her. She opened her eyes and they were face-to-face. He moved forward and kissed her deeply, their lips twining in an age-old passionate rhythm, her bare breasts pressed against the crisp hair on his chest. Maura returned Doug's feverish kisses with a passion completely new to her. This was it, she suddenly thought in some distant part of her mind. This is what it's meant to be like between a man and a woman. Every romance she'd had before—even believing herself truly in love with Scott Walker—seemed a pale, watered-down imitation.

She realized that from the very start of her relationship with Doug this was what she had always wanted. To be held in his strong arms, to feel his powerful body against hers, to revel in his intimate touch. To allow herself to open up to him, like a flower opening to the heat of the sun. To feel her very soul laid bare to him.

Then his mouth moved from her lips to her neck and lower, exploring the soft curve of her breasts until she thought she'd cry out with pleasure as he covered first one taut nipple then the other. Maura's eyes squeezed closed, her body thrilled with exquisite satisfaction. Her hands gripped his muscular shoulders, gliding over the firm muscle and warm skin.

Finally he stopped, his head pressed into the hollow of her breasts. She felt him breathe deeply, struggling for control.

"God, you're so beautiful, Maura. How could you ever think I'd feel shortchanged? I want you so much." His voice sounded raw with desire.

Maura couldn't reply. Did he really think she was beautiful? Her? A total plain Jane if there ever was one? But she didn't think he was lying to her, just saying what he thought she wanted to hear. She truly felt beautiful in his arms, beautiful and desirable. It was unbelievable but true. That was the effect he had on her.

She buried her face in his thick hair and wrapped her arms around his strong back. She felt his hands on her thighs, slipping under the edge of her thin nightgown, the pressure of his touch unnerving and totally tantalizing.

Then he lifted his head and stared straight into her eyes. With his hands on her hips, he pulled her closer, so that she sat at the edge of the chair, her legs slipping around his waist, her warm feminine core pressed against his lower body in a way that left no doubt as to his urgent desire. When he moved his hips, Maura moved against him. He sighed and kissed her deeply, and she felt his body shudder in her arms.

"Maura, if you don't want this to happen, it's okay," he whispered against her lips. "Tell me now, so we can stop."

Maura's head dropped against his shoulder, her body throbbing with longing, the feelings so powerful she could hardly think, no less answer him.

Was there any point in turning him away tonight? From the first time he'd kissed her, she'd secretly felt that sooner or later they would make love. No matter how many times she'd denied it to herself. Not to mention that they were now husband and wife.

Still, she'd never expected his merest touch would send her up in flames. But here she was, totally on fire for him. All she wanted to do right now was show him how he made her feel and how much she wanted him, too. Maybe it wasn't the right thing to do. Maybe she would end up regretting surrendering herself to those feelings. But right now she just couldn't resist.

He tightened his hold on her, silently urging her reply. Maura lifted her head very slightly, her lips just grazing his ear. "Come to my room. The bed is much bigger,'' she whispered. Her seductive tone was totally unfamiliar to her, but it definitely felt good.

"So I've noticed," he admitted with a low, sexy laugh.

She met his gaze and felt herself blush at his grin and then blush more when he pressed a hot kiss into the valley between her breasts and lifted the straps of her nightgown back up to her shoulders. Seconds later she was lost in another deep, devouring kiss as Doug stood up and pulled her up off her seat with him.

In her bedroom they kissed again and with Doug's mouth pressed against hers, Maura felt herself falling in his embrace down to her bed, where they landed, their bodies a tangle of arms and legs.

While his mouth worked tender magic on the taut peaks of her breasts, his hands magically smoothed away her nightgown and lacy underpants. Maura's fingers worked on the clasp and zipper of his jeans, and Doug moaned with a mixture of pleasure and frustration at her tantalizing touch. He pulled away for just an instant to shuck off his pants and throw them to the floor. Then he moved back toward her, covering her body with his, and she luxuriated in the feel of him pressing down on her, his bare, hair-roughened skin covering every inch of her, his muscular thigh pressed between her legs. No man had ever made her feel so sensual, so desired. She wanted to taste and touch every inch of him, and as her hands caressed his powerful shoulders and back, her lips pressed warm kisses to his chest. She found one flat male nipple and twirled her tongue around the hardened bud.

Doug groaned his satisfaction and pulled her close,

his hardened manhood pressing against her thigh. "Doug," she sighed, shifting her hips to let him know she was ready for him to make them one.

"Not yet," he murmured. "I spent some long lonely nights in that spare room of yours, Maura. Too long to rush now."

Then his body backed up his words. His mouth laved her breasts and his hand smoothed down the length of her body in a slow, sensuous exploration of each curve. As his questing fingers moved even lower, to the source of her heat, Maura couldn't speak, she couldn't even think. Swept away on a sea of pure sensation, she felt her body rise and dip as Doug's loving touch brought her to the keenest edge of pleasure.

Finally her arms urged him closer and he moved over her, ready to satisfy her completely. She circled his lean hips with her long legs and felt his beating heart close to hers as he moved inside her. His body seemed to fit hers perfectly, and his passionate power overwhelmed her. As she matched and met his rhythm she felt them merge in a deep, mystical way. Something incredible and beyond description.

Her eyes squeezed shut as she reached her peak, her mind exploding with heat and light, her body trembling in his arms. She felt him move against her one last time and then explode with a cry of satisfaction as he called her name.

She held him close against her, feeling as if they were both tumbling out of the sky, and she knew that after tonight she would never be the same. She had let him into her heart and her body. Now he was part of her, in her very breath, her blood and her soul.

* * *

As they drove to the Connelly mansion in Doug's tiny sports car, Maura stared straight ahead, her hands clasped in her lap. She suddenly hated the navy-blue linen suit she had on. The outfit had always been one of her favorites, but now she realized just how long it had been hanging in her closet. She felt so dull and hopelessly out of style.

The Connellys would think Doug had married a dowdy little nurse. And once they found out she was pregnant, they'd think she'd trapped him. They weren't going to like her. Not at all. She could feel it in her bones...

Should she ask Doug to turn back to the house so she could change? But what would she change into? She hated clothes shopping and her closet looked it. So far Doug hadn't seem to notice her wardrobe—or lack of it. Ever since the other night, when he'd surprised her in the kitchen, they had spent every spare minute together making love. The only thing he'd seen her in lately was a bed sheet.

She glanced over at his rugged profile, his eyes intent on the road, his strong hands gripping the wheel. No, she couldn't ask him to turn around. It was too silly. But her hair—that was wrong too. She took a brush out of her purse and started working on it, intent on pulling it back with a clip in her usual style.

"Your hair looks fine, Maura." Doug glanced over at her and then back at the road. "You're going to wear out that brush if you change it one more time."

"I'll feel better with it back. Not so messy," she insisted as she fastened the clip.

"You look great," he assured her for at least the tenth time since they'd started out. "It's just brunch with my family. Not an audience with the queen of England."

"I'm sorry...I'm just nervous. And your stepmother might not be a queen but she is a princess," she pointed out.

He glanced her way again, his expression sympathetic. "I know you feel a bit shy sometimes, Maura. But believe me, there's no reason to feel intimidated. They're just regular people."

"Right, just regular folks. If you forget about the mansion, the yacht, the private jet, their world-famous name and their millions," Maura said dryly. "Sure, they're just like everyone else I know."

Doug laughed. "Okay, I get your point. But you act as if I'm sending you out to a firing squad." He took her hand and held it tight. "You're not going in there all alone. You're with me, remember?"

She met his glance and finally smiled. He was right. Doug would be with her every second. She was letting her natural shyness get the best of her. Wasn't it time she outgrew that problem? Feeling Doug's firm grasp, she resolved that today would be the day.

They'd left the highway and were driving through an area of expensive houses and estates, she noticed. The road was narrow and lined with tall trees. Only the roadside mailboxes and large gates indicated that a home existed somewhere behind the woodsy landscape. It wouldn't be long now before Doug turned up one of the private estate roads. She felt her stomach knot with nerves.

Now she would meet his family, and they'd play

the part of the happy newlyweds. Just as they did at
the hospital, where everyone accepted the news of
their sudden marriage with far less shock and comment than she'd ever expected.

She stole another secret glance at Doug. He wore
a black linen sports jacket with a black knit shirt and
gunmetal gray trousers made of some expensive-
looking fabric. He looked very sophisticated...and
much too handsome. It was easy to pretend to be in
love with him. Maybe she wasn't just pretending anymore, Maura realized. For better or worse, whether
this marriage worked out or it didn't, she was quickly
and steadily falling in love with her husband.

They finally drove up to the Connellys' red brick
Georgian mansion, and with the house in full view,
Maura seriously considered making a run for it. But
of course she couldn't escape now. Besides, Doug had
pocketed the car keys much too quickly for her to
manage a quick getaway.

A servant opened the door and greeted Doug by
name. Then Emma and Grant Connelly immediately
appeared. As they stood in the huge entryway making
small talk, she wasn't sure how she got through the
introductions. As much as she tried to focus on Grant
and Emma's conversation, her mind was spinning
from the sheer luxury and vastness of her surround-
ings. Outside of the movies, Maura had never seen a
home like this one before. Astounding, distracting
sights came into view everywhere she turned—original paintings, sculpture, antique oriental rugs. Even
the architectural detail of doorway columns, mantels
and the marble flooring and carved moldings was distracting.

But once they settled in the living room for cock-
tails, Maura was able to relax and focus on the conversation. Doug had been right. His stepmother,
Emma, and his father, Grant, were a warm, down-to-
earth couple.

Despite his wealth and influence, Grant Connelly
had no pretensions or snobbery. He was handsome
and distinguished, even more so than his photographs.
But his gaze and manner were far warmer and per-
sonable than his reputation as a corporate mogul suggested.

Emma was beautiful, so poised and gracious,
Maura thought. Regal down to her elegant fingertips.
Her engaging manner quickly put Maura at ease. Like
most people with excellent social skills, she didn't
talk about herself at all but asked Maura questions
about herself, how she had met Doug and about her
specialty in pediatrics.

Just as Doug had predicted, Emma and Grant soon
mentioned that they wanted to throw a party to celebrate their son's marriage. Maura tried to look
pleased, but she knew the flash of worry on her face
had not escaped Emma's notice.

"Don't worry, dear. It will just be the family and
some close friends," she promised her. "Everybody's
so eager to meet you."

"We thought a barbecue at the lake house would
be fun," Grant added. "We can just relax and visit
and do as we please."

"Sounds good to me," Doug said, glancing at
Maura. "We'll be there." He squeezed Maura's hand,
and she smiled her agreement. But she secretly won-

dered if she was up to a repeat of today's performance, in front of an even larger audience.

When the meal was over, Emma invited Maura for a walk through the grounds. Doug would have some time visiting with his father alone.

The gardens were beautiful and arranged in a formal style. Emma showed her the maze formed out of boxwood shrubs where her many children used to play.

"I'm looking forward to chasing some grandchildren through there someday," she added with smile.

Maura felt herself blush, but made no reply. Had Emma guessed that she was expecting? No, that seemed impossible. Everyone says that sort of thing to newlyweds, Maura reminded herself.

"We just added this rose garden last spring," Emma noted as they passed a beautiful garden laid out in a circular design with graveled paths and a stone fountain at the center. "I'd love to get some really huge blooms this year. Last year it was so rainy the flowers practically drowned," Emma noted with a laugh.

"My mother used to feed the roses eggshells," Maura recalled. "She said they liked calcium." Then she suddenly felt silly passing along the household hint to a woman like Emma, who of course would have the best gardener money could buy tending her roses.

"Yes, I've heard that before. I think I'll try it this year," Emma replied thoughtfully. "You sound as if you know something about flowers. Do you garden, Maura?"

She shook her head. "Doug and I are in an apartment now. With my work hours there's really no time for it, anyway.''

"There'll be plenty of time. Before you know it, you and Doug will be starting a family and buying a house and so on and so on,'' she predicted with a laugh. "One thing just leads to another.''

"We've only been at my place about a week,'' Maura replied with a small smile. "Doug hasn't even unpacked all his things yet.''

"Yes, I'm sure you're both just getting used to each other. Marriage isn't easy,'' she added with a small knowing smile. "But you look very happy together. I haven't known Doug for very long, but I've never seen him happier,'' she said with sincerity. "He really can't take his eyes off you, dear. Enjoy it,'' Emma added in a playful whisper.

Maura felt herself blush again, now even more than before. She didn't know what to say. She had felt Doug glowing with attention and praise for her all afternoon, but she had to keep reminding herself that it was all just a performance for his family. On his part, at least.

As they headed back to the house, Emma reached out and took Maura's arm in an affectionate way. Maura felt surprised at first, then warmed by the gesture. This was what it was like to be with family, she realized. This feeling of warmth and acceptance. It had been so long since she'd experienced it.

Finally it was time to go. Grant and Emma each hugged her in turn, and then Grant put his arm around Maura again. He turned to Doug and said, "When you called last week and told us you'd eloped, well…we were surprised, to say the least. But now that we've met Maura, we can see what all the rush was about. You wouldn't want to let a girl like this get away.''

Maura thought she saw her husband's cheek flush under his bronze complexion. But he quickly disguised any embarrassment with a deep laugh. There were more goodbyes and finally, they were alone in Doug's car, driving back to their apartment.

After a long silence Doug said, ''Now, that wasn't so bad, was it?''

''They're great. Just the way you described them,'' she said brightly. ''Still, it was a bit stressful meeting the real live Connellys,'' she admitted.

''Maybe you need a massage when we get home,'' he offered in an innocent tone. He reached over and lightly touched her nape with his fingertips. The contact was enough to send shock waves reverberating through her body. Along with the searing memory of his last massage...and what happened afterward.

Maura felt her body temperature rise at the mere memory.

''Hmm...'' She leaned her head back on the seat and closed her eyes. ''Maybe it's my turn to give you one,'' she suggested softly. ''Nurses are very good at that sort of thing, you know.''

''Yes, I've heard that,'' Doug murmured. Maura felt the car instantly accelerate. Doug sat up straight in his seat, his attention suddenly focused on the road.

She sat up, too, and glanced at him. ''Something the matter?''

''Not at all,'' he assured her. ''Check your seat belt. I think I just remembered a shortcut home.''

* * *

Grant and Emma didn't take long to agree that Doug had chosen a wonderful young woman to be his wife. "It was sudden," Grant said thoughtfully, "but they look perfect together."

"Yes, they do, don't they? She's lovely," Emma said, "and she seems devoted to him."

"As he does to her," Grant noted. He knew that his son Doug had been through so much pain and loss in the past few years, with the betrayal of his wife and the loss of his mother. It was hard for him to trust and reveal his feelings, even to those closest to him. But Grant felt certain that Doug was truly in love with Maura. He hoped that love would go a long way toward ensuring his son's happiness.

"What more could a man ask for?" Emma offered. "She's beautiful, intelligent, sensitive—"

"She sounds great. When can I meet her?" a familiar voice asked with a deep, sexy laugh.

"Seth, what a nice surprise." Emma smiled at her stepson as he leaned to kiss her on the cheek. "Grant, you didn't tell me Seth was stopping by today."

"I didn't know," Grant said honestly. "Too bad you didn't come sooner. You just missed Doug and his new bride."

"Too bad. I wanted to congratulate him," Seth said. "Were you just exchanging notes about his wife when I came in? She sounds terrific."

"She is," Emma replied. "Maybe when you meet her you'll decide marriage isn't such a bad idea after all."

Seth laughed. "I never said marriage was a bad idea. I only said I wasn't ready and don't think I will be for a time."

"Spoken like a true attorney," Emma shot back with a grin.

"Spoken like a true mother," Seth teased in return. "Here, Dad. Here's the paperwork you wanted." He then mentioned an important deal he'd been working on for the company and handed Grant a thick manila envelope.

"Thanks, I've been waiting to see this," Grant said as he took the package from Seth's hand.

"By the way, I had someone look into the product you told me about."

Seth frowned for a moment, then his expression brightened. "Sure, the lace company in Altaria. Angie's father, Ed, told me about it. Port Royal Textile, I think the name was. He just asked me the other day if we were going to take any action. What do you think?"

"Charlotte did some research on the company," Grant said, mentioning his assistant, Charlotte Masters. "The report was very favorable. They seem like a solid outfit and their product is outstanding. I'm going to pursue it. I'm not sure yet when the actual shipments will start and how fast we can market the product. But the firm seems quite easy to deal with so far. It shouldn't be too long."

"Sounds good. I'll have to thank Ed for the tip," Seth said.

"Do you see Angie often?" Emma asked, curious to hear about Seth's new relationship with his birth mother.

"We've met for dinner or lunch a few times and keep in touch by phone," he explained. "She wanted me to meet her father, Ed. 'Your grandad,' she always calls him," Seth added with a laugh. "It's been good to get to know her. And difficult at times, too," he admitted, breaking Emma's gaze for a moment. "We've talked about the past, and Angie seems very sorry for not being...well, not being the greatest parent in the world." Grant was surprised to hear that Angie had apologized and could see that Emma had the same reaction. "Just hearing her apology has meant a lot to me. I really think she's changed a great deal from those years when she was raising me all alone. She didn't have it very easy then, either," he added sympathetically.

"No, she didn't," Grant agreed.

He'd once felt quite sorry for Angie Donahue and responsible for her, as well. But for a long time he'd come to see her as the type of person who created a lot of her own problems and typically pushed the responsibility off on someone else.

He didn't want to voice any negatives about Angie to Seth, especially not now. Maybe she'd changed, he reflected. Who was he to judge her?

"That's good, Seth," Emma said, reaching out to take his hand. "I'm glad that you got in touch with her and it's going so well. You're very generous to forgive her," she added. "You know what they say, it's good for the soul."

Grant glanced over at Emma, a woman who knew about forgiveness, if ever there was one. He could only imagine how torn she felt, having this conversation. But as always she rose admirably to the moment, her first concern for her stepson Seth, whom she loved as dearly as any of her natural-born children.

Seth returned Emma's gaze, easing the moment with his charming smile. "You worry too much," he said kindly.

"Well, until you find a wife to look out for you, looks like you're stuck with me," Emma replied with a wry grin.

"Watch out, son," Grant warned, as he slipped on his reading glasses, "she's on a roll."

Seth's handsome features struggled to suppress a grin. "Wow, look at the time," he said suddenly. "Nice seeing you, folks. Looks like I've got to go."

Maura opened her eyes to find Doug's face on the pillow beside her. The room was dark, and it slowly came back to her, how they'd stumbled into the house after the car ride, leaving a trail of clothes from the front door to the bed. After making love, they had fallen into a deep, contented sleep in each other's arms.

She held very still, studying the lines of his rugged features, his wide, smooth brow, high cheekbones and strong, blunt chin. She had the urge to trace each one with her fingertip but didn't want to wake him.

Her heart ached just to look at him. Almost all afternoon at his parents' home he'd stuck by her side like glue, his amber gaze filled with pride and affection. He'd acted the role of a newlywed groom to perfection, she thought. Time and again she had to remind herself it was only an act.

But for her part it was different. Far different now, Maura knew. How had he become so dear to her so quickly? She couldn't say. Sometimes she wondered if she'd always had deep feelings for him, simmering just below the surface of their friendship. Feelings she never dared to acknowledge.

It was a mystery. But now an undeniable truth. She was falling in love with him.

She was besieged by feelings, feelings that were different from any she'd ever known before. Utterly terrifying and unbearably wonderful at the same time. But it was important to remember that while he eagerly shared her bed and enjoyed her body, in his heart he didn't feel the same about her.

Though he'd done his best the other night to dispel her fears, there was still a good chance their impulsive marriage wouldn't last. Maura didn't like to dwell on that dark possibility. But it couldn't be avoided. All she could do was wait and watch…and hope that someday Doug would truly love her. Could she stay in this marriage, knowing she loved him but he didn't feel the same?

Doug's eyes slowly opened, and he smiled at her. "I thought I felt someone staring at me. See anything you like?"

She laughed at his uncharacteristic vanity.

"Sorry, not at all." She forced a serious expression. "I was just wondering how I got stuck with such an unattractive man."

He laughed and reached out, snagging one of her long curls with his finger. "I talked you into it, remember?"

"Yes, you did make a convincing pitch." She smiled and slid back, sitting up against the pillows, the sheet clinging to her bare breasts.

"Having second thoughts again?" His tone was still teasing, yet she sensed a true note of concern.

"Not at all." She met his gaze and held it. He was the first to look away.

"I know we promised not to talk about it, but do you ever think about Scott anymore? You can be honest with me," he added. "I won't get mad."

"No, never," Maura answered without missing a beat. "If I do, it's probably not the way you mean. I only think about how stupid I was to get taken in by him," she said with an edge of bitterness and anger at herself.

"Maura, I'm sorry," Doug moved closer and put his arm around her shoulder. "I shouldn't have brought it up."

Maura sighed and rested her head against Doug's shoulder. She felt instantly better in his embrace.

"What about you?" she asked after a long moment. "Do you ever think about your first marriage? You've never really told me anything about it. I don't even know her name."

"Her name was Karen." She waited, expecting him to say more. But he didn't.

He shifted slightly, and she could tell that it was hard for him to talk about it. She almost said, hey, it's okay, it can wait until another time. But she was too curious. She needed to know what went wrong. At times she sensed that Doug had been deeply hurt by that relationship, wounded in a way that would make it hard for him to ever love again. She needed to know if she even had a chance of scaling the walls around his heart.

"We met in college," he began slowly. "She was bright, fun and very beautiful. Every guy I knew wanted to go out with her. For some reason she picked me. We were as opposite as two people could be. I was really into the books. I knew I needed more scholarship money to go to medical school and I was determined to do it. Karen's family was very wealthy. She grew up in Lake Forest and she had no real ambition beyond being some rich man's wife. She liked the idea of being married to a doctor,'' he added with a sharp edge to his tone. ''At least, at first she did.

''But it didn't turn out the way she'd planned. She had imagined a guy with a pleasant little suburban practice, treating kids with the usual sore throats and stomach viruses. Coming home at five and then fulfilling her busy social calendar. Dinners out in town or golf at the country club. She didn't like her husband caring for the inner-city poor. She didn't like the fact that my hours were unpredictable and my priorities might cut into some doubles match or ski weekend she'd planned for us.''

He paused, and she felt his entire body grow tense beside her.

''I understand. You don't have to say more.''

''No, you asked. Let me get this over with, once and for all,'' he insisted in a low, grating tone that made her stomach knot with dread. ''There isn't much more to the story, actually. When Karen figured out that she couldn't pressure me into being the kind of husband—and the kind of doctor—she wanted, she traded me in a for a more suitable model. She had an affair with a guy I roomed with in med school, a plastic surgeon.''

''I'm sorry.'' Maura lifted her head and met his gaze. ''That must have been devastating for you.''

''It was at first. I'd been hiding in my work,'' he

admitted, "and I felt blindsided by the news. But I had to face that there wasn't much of a marriage left. If there ever had been anything real between us at all."

He took a deep breath, wondering if he should tell Maura about how he wanted a baby and Karen didn't. That had caused their marriage to fall apart as much as anything, he knew. And he had to tell Maura, sooner or later, the real reason he'd married her. One of the real reasons...

He glanced down at her, feeling the words on the tip of his tongue. But as he stared into her soulful, trusting gaze, he felt his mouth grow dry as chalk. The words just couldn't come. He swallowed hard and looked away.

"It was all for the best," he said finally. "Karen got married again right after the divorce. Bought a big place up in Lake Forest, not far from her parents' home. She's very happy, I hear."

As she'd guessed, his ex-wife had hurt him deeply, and he was still very angry. But was Doug still in love with her, despite the way she'd hurt him? Maura wondered. Karen sounded exactly like the type that drove men crazy. Doug had claimed that wasn't what he wanted. But maybe it really was. Maura knew she could never compete with that type of woman—or even her memory.

"It's hard to talk about these things," Maura said quietly. "Thank you for telling me about it."

He held her, saying nothing for a long time. She felt his hand stroking her hair.

Then he said, "I don't think about Karen at all

anymore, Maura, if that's what you're wondering. We had nothing in common, really, when you get right down to it. We could barely talk to each other. Not like you and me.''

His reply was reassuring. Yet Maura wasn't quite sure what he meant. Did he simply mean that they were good friends? ''Because I understand your work, you mean?'' she asked.

''Well, yes. It's hard to explain exactly...'' His deep voice trailed off. She felt his heartbeat, strong and steady under her hand.

He hadn't said he loved her. Far from it. But he was satisfied with their marriage. Maybe because he *wasn't* in love with her, Maura thought with a twinge of pain. He'd been hurt so deeply by his ex-wife, maybe he would never really recover enough to truly love again. Could she live with that, she wondered? She wasn't sure. She didn't feel sure of anything right now and wondered if it had been a mistake after all to give in to her feelings of attraction and make love to Doug.

She felt his strong hand on her cheek, turning her to face him. ''Don't you think it's working out between us?'' he asked.

''Yes...it works,'' she replied quietly. She knew he meant they got along day to day—and the lovemaking was extraordinary. Meanwhile, she wanted to talk about something far different, but couldn't dare say: I never imagined that night you proposed, that I'd fall in love with you so deeply and so fast. Too bad it looks like you can never love me.

His hand slid into her hair and his smile widened.

"I had a feeling it would work out. And I had my fantasies," he admitted, his voice low and rough.

"Fantasies? About me?" she whispered into the curve of his shoulder. How could anyone have fantasies about her? She shook her head and broke her gaze from his.

He must just be saying that, she told herself. Still, the idea was very flattering, and exciting.

"Yes, definitely," he insisted. "Does that embarrass you?"

"Uh, no. I mean, yes," she confessed. Then, feeling just too curious to let it drop, she said, "Like for instance…?"

His soft, sexy laugh excited her even more, and his body moved restlessly against hers with tantalizing, sensual friction.

"For instance…let me show you…" And before she could even murmur her reply, his mouth covered hers in a deep, hard kiss, and his hands glided possessively over her soft curves.

He pulled her closer under the sheet so that their bodies were pressed together, hip to hip. She felt his long muscular legs tangle with hers and knew he was ready to make love again.

Maura surrendered once again to the sensual magic of Doug's touch and the overpowering passion that ignited so quickly between them. It was easy to forget that he'd never said the words she wanted to hear. That he was thinking only about how good it was for them in bed. Astounding, actually. And all he would admit to feeling for her was a mixture of friendship and sexual chemistry, when she was feeling much more.

His hands caressed her body with a newfound knowledge of her secret pleasure points and an eagerness to discover new ones. Her mouth merged with his in a deep, soulful kiss, and she knew she could never resist him...or resist having him as her own for however long their marriage lasted.

Five

Bright and early on Saturday morning Maura stood outside her apartment waiting for the Connelly limousine to arrive. She couldn't believe she had agreed to go on this outing with Emma Connelly and her daughters. But here she was.

When Emma had called a few nights ago and invited her to meet her daughters, Maura had felt intimidated by the idea. But she'd also thought it would be too rude to refuse. She assumed Emma meant they'd meet for lunch out, or perhaps at the Connelly mansion again. She'd be on her own this time, without Doug. But how hard would it be to make small talk with Emma and her daughters for an hour or so?

But Emma's plans were a bit more involved. She was, after all, a princess, Maura reminded herself. Emma wanted to introduce Maura to Alexandra, Tara and Maggie. She was also going to invite Jennifer Anderson, her social secretary, who had recently become engaged to Doug's brother, Chance. The two couples had spoken over the phone but hadn't met yet since their schedules were both so busy.

The group was booked for an entire day of beauty treatments at the Golden Palm, Chicago's most exclusive spa. "Then after lunch I thought we'd go over to Carrington Plaza for some shopping," Emma added cheerfully.

Carrington Plaza? Maura had read about the fantastic collection of exclusive designer shops in magazines, but had never dared set foot inside. She knew she couldn't afford as much as a belt in one of those places. And she couldn't even pronounce half the exotic names of the designers.

Well, it couldn't hurt to look, she thought. Even if she didn't buy anything.

"And guess what?" Emma continued. "When I mentioned the outing to Grant, he insisted on treating everyone."

"How generous," Maura said. Now she had no excuses left to decline.

"The girls loved the idea. They're really all so excited to meet you."

"I'm eager to meet them, too," Maura said honestly.

So it had been settled. But when Maura had told Doug about it, she hadn't been able to hide her nervousness at meeting his stepsisters. He'd tried not to laugh, but finally couldn't help himself.

"Maura, for goodness sake, you sound as if they

plan to boil you in oil. I really think all Emma has in mind is a manicure and maybe a haircut.''

''I'm just not the day-spa type, in case you hadn't noticed.''

''Thank goodness for that.'' With an indulgent smile Doug took hold of her shoulders and gazed into her eyes. ''You can have a day out and pamper yourself a little. You work so hard. And you'll have even less time after the baby comes for this type of thing.'' He pulled out a credit card and forced it into her hand. ''I want you to come home with a big shopping bag of stuff. A present from me. Anything you like,'' he urged her.

Maura took the card in her hand and stared down at it, as if she'd never seen one before. Suddenly everybody wanted to buy her things. She simply wasn't used to all the attention.

''I guess I could look for something to wear to your parents' party,'' Maura replied, feeling moved by his generosity. ''Do you think a dress would be okay? Or something more casual?''

''You look great in anything,'' he insisted. He kissed her softly and smiled into her eyes. ''You look great in nothing, too—'' His hands wandered down to her hips ''—come to think of it...''

She knew that tone by now and felt her body growing warm all over in response.

''Doug, I have to get over to the hospital,'' she reminded him as his mouth moved down to the sensitive spot just below her ear. Doug didn't seem to hear her. Or if he did, he didn't care if she was late. Very soon even she forgot about getting to work on time, and they had made love with urgent need.

Their work hours had not coincided much this week and Maura felt an aching hunger for his lovemaking. She'd become addicted to him—his touch, his taste, the scent of his warm skin. It was hard to last even a day without having him near her.

Now here she was, at barely half past seven, about to embark on her first spa adventure, when she'd much rather be back upstairs in bed with Doug.

Just then a long white limo pulled up in front her apartment building, dispelling her erotic daydreams. The driver hopped out and opened the rear passenger door. Maura peeked in, and the first person she saw was Emma Connelly, dressed in a spring-green silk suit.

"Good morning, Maura," Emma greeted her. "You're our last stop. Come in, have a seat." She indicated the place next to her. "These are my daughters, Alexandra, Tara and Maggie," she said once Maura was seated. She introduced three beautiful young women sitting on the opposite side of the car. "Jennifer Anderson will meet us at the spa," Emma noted.

Maura said good morning and settled herself on the long leather seat next to Emma. Emma's daughters had the same warmth and social graces as their mother and immediately helped her feel at ease. Within a few blocks from home Maura felt comfortable and welcomed by them.

The interior of the car was almost as big as her living room, she noticed, as she stretched out her legs. On a wet bar near Emma, she saw coffee in a silver server, croissants and a crystal dish of huge strawberries.

Well, you're with the Connellys now, she reminded herself. As Doug had often told her, better get used to it.

"Ready for our day out?" Emma asked brightly.

"As ready as I'll ever be," Maura replied with a smile.

As the long limo carried her home that evening, Maura sank back into the seat, exhausted. She'd had no idea that pampering herself would be such hard work.

Doug's stepsisters had been terrific company and had made her feel as if she were a long-lost relative who had finally returned home. She'd also gotten to know Jennifer Anderson, her future sister-in-law. They'd had some fun, one-on-one, comparing private notes on Chance and Doug.

Despite her natural shyness with strangers, Maura had soon relaxed and opened up and enjoyed a certain kind of camaraderie and fun that could only happen in the company of other women. She almost felt as if she was back in college, hanging out with her dorm pals. Only, in those days their nights of beauty treatments followed homemade recipes from magazines— potions like egg white and oatmeal facials.

At the spa the ingredients were far more exotic and outrageously expensive. She'd been buffed and polished, scrubbed with herbal extracts and soothed with vitamin-enriched lotions. She'd been wrapped in seaweed and then massaged into a state of total, mindless relaxation, inhaling intense scents designed to soothe and invigorate.

And that was just the beautification warm-up.

Maura was surprised to hear that Emma had also scheduled her for a marathon session in the salon. "Just the usual," Emma said casually, when Maura's eyes widened.

She'd had a facial and a manicure, then a pedicure that in fact *had* included a foot soak in hot oils. She'd be sure to tell Doug about that.

Even though Maura hadn't want anything special done to her long hair, somehow Emma and her girls had persuaded her to experiment. She wasn't sure now how she'd been talked into it. But before she knew it, she'd been rinsed with something that brought out the gold and red highlights and then had a haircut.

Her stomach knotted in dread as she saw chunks of her hair hit the floor. But it all happened so fast, and she felt silly protesting right in the middle of it.

But when all was said and done, not nearly as much length was lost as she'd thought. Her natural curls were cut in different lengths so that her thick hair bounced up more, creating a halo effect around her oval face.

After it was blown out and finished, Maura admired the style with surprise. Doug loved her hair down loose and now it looked so much better the new way. But it was still long enough to pull back for work.

Maura had thought she would escape the makeup consultant. She never wore makeup and didn't even have time for it most days, she'd protested. But her new pals had again persuaded her to give it a chance. The salon expert had known she was wary and had used a sensitive approach, and when it was all over, Maura actually thought her "new face" was something she could do on her own, though the subtle touches to her eyes and lips made a dramatic difference in her looks.

Maura had felt pleased but definitely relieved when the group finally left the spa. They'd stopped for lunch at a beautiful restaurant that was filled with flowers. Maura was seated next to Jennifer, giving her a chance to get to know her future sister-in-law a bit. Jennifer was as sweet as she was lovely. She looked far too young to Maura to be a widow, but Jennifer's husband, a police officer, had lost his life in the line of duty two years ago. She'd been pregnant at the time. She'd been raising her little girl, Sarah, on her own. That was, until she'd met Chance.

"Chance was totally shocked when Doug told him he'd eloped," Jennifer had confided. "I thought he was going to faint. He had no idea Doug was even seeing anybody."

"It was just very…sudden. We were really just friends for the longest time," Maura tried to explain. She always hated when she was put in this position, having to lie about her relationship with Doug. But there didn't seem to be any way around it.

"I thought it was really romantic," Jennifer confided. "Even though I had to scratch Doug's name off my list for the bachelor auction."

Emma laughed, but Maura didn't quite understand the joke.

"Jennifer is organizing a bachelor auction for a local charity. She's having trouble rounding up enough handsome, eligible men. Any suggestions, girls?" Emma asked her daughters.

"How about Justin?" Alexandra suggested, offering up her younger brother. ''Have you asked him yet?''

''No, I haven't. Do you think he'll do it?'' Jennifer asked. ''I asked Seth and he claims he'll be out of town. But I could tell he was just looking for some polite excuse.''

''Maybe if Mom asks him,'' Tara said, glancing at her mother.

''Of course he'll do it. It's for a very worthy cause,'' Emma insisted as she pulled out her cell phone and dialed. ''And it will be good for him to get out and have some fun. Ever since he took over Daniel's job, he's been working much too hard. I don't even think he's dating anyone right now. It's just work, work, work. I bet he's at the office as we speak, on a Saturday. See, what did I tell you? He's picking up,'' she whispered with her hand over the mouthpiece.

Then she turned her attention from the table to the phone and greeted her son. They spoke briefly, and Maura could tell from Emma's side of the conversation that though Justin was reluctant to be auctioned off even for charity, he couldn't refuse his mother's request.

''Thank you, dear,'' Emma said. ''All right, I'll tell Jennifer to call your secretary with the details. I do hope you manage to get out of the office for some part of the weekend, Justin. I'm going to check on you, too,'' she warned him.

When Emma completed the call, Jennifer was pleased to add Justin's name to her list and thanked Emma repeatedly. She also promised Emma that there would be plenty of beautiful, successful single women at the event and Justin wouldn't stay unattached for long.

But Justin's sisters were full of wry comments about their hardworking brother. They weren't sure what type of woman would catch Justin's eye. "But if she had a calculator implanted somewhere on her body, it wouldn't hurt," Tara joked, which sent the others into a fresh wave of laughter.

After lunch the group had moved on to a shopping spree at Carrington Plaza. Again, Maura had felt like a giddy sorority girl, as she and the Connelly sisters virtually took over the dressing rooms in each exclusive boutique, running in and out of each other's rooms to trade clothes and model outfits. Maura was easily caught up in the fun and, with a little encouragement, found herself buying several new outfits.

None of the women had guessed that she was pregnant, however. Maura was certain of it. Her figure had hardly changed at all yet, and certainly not in any way that a stranger would notice. Her choice in clothing tended toward the loose, baggy look anyway.

She chose a formfitting sheath for the barbecue with a scooped neckline and straps that tied on each shoulder. The style of the dress was deceptively simple, but the unusual fabric made it a knockout. The floral pattern in sea blue and gold seemed painted by some master and went perfectly with Maura's coloring. She almost thought it was too dressy, but Emma and her daughters "oohed" and "ahhed" and had so many compliments when Maura modeled it for them, that she couldn't leave the gorgeous designer dress behind.

Maura had stared at her reflection. She couldn't

help it. She looked completely different from the woman who had left her apartment that very morning—from her new hairdo down to the tips of her polished toes.

"Wow, you look great in that, Maura," Alexandra exclaimed.

"Wait till Doug sees you," Maggie warned.

Would he even recognize her? Maura wondered, checking her view from the side.

"That was made for you, dear," Emma insisted. "Please permit me get it for you. Think of it as a little gift for the bride from me and Grant. You didn't even get a bridal shower, you know," Emma reminded her.

While Maura had protested, Emma wouldn't hear of it. Maura finally accepted the dress graciously, thinking how wonderful it was to be part of a family again. The day of luxury had been something special. But for Maura the most precious part had been feeling a bond with the Connelly women.

It was nearly six o'clock when Maura got home. Doug was out and she wasn't sure when he'd be back. She carried her shopping bags straight to the bedroom. The sun was just starting to set, bathing her room in warm, hazy light.

She hung up a few new articles of clothing, feeling a bit disappointed. She'd been anticipating Doug's reaction to her makeover and now he wasn't even home. She picked up the new dress she'd chosen for the barbecue and held it against herself as she looked in the mirror. Why did this always happen to her? The clothes she bought looked so good in the store, but when she got them home, she couldn't imagine what she'd been thinking.

The dress was beautiful. But was it too much for her. Now, after Emma and her daughters had seen it, she really had to wear it for the party. But what if she looked silly in it? What if Doug was embarrassed?

Full of buyer's remorse, Maura decided to try it on one more time before she put it away. She had to stand on a chair in order to see her full reflection in the mirror over her dresser. She was just checking out the length when she caught sight of Doug standing in the doorway.

She turned to face him, noticing the shocked expression on his face. "Doug…is something wrong?"

"You shouldn't be standing on a chair like that, Maura. You could hurt yourself—and the baby."

"Oh, of course." Maura hadn't even thought of that. She started to get down and he was instantly at her side, reaching out to grip her waist. She placed her hands on his shoulders, and as he lifted her down, her body pressed sensuously along the length of his, sending a current of pure heat arcing through her.

"I…I was just checking out this dress. I'm not sure if I should keep it."

For some reason the way he was looking at her made her nervous. He was staring at her like a total stranger might, as if he'd never seen her before. His unreadable expression gave no clue as to whether or not he liked what he saw.

"Emma sort of insisted," she explained, her voice shaking nervously. "Do you like it?"

He was silent for a long moment. He didn't even look at the dress. Or if he had, she hadn't noticed.

"It's great. Take it off." His tone was low, barely audible. He pushed her hair aside roughly, and his mouth pressed hotly against the soft skin on her shoulder. His touch instantly excited her, and it was hard for Maura to keep her mind clear.

"You don't like it, do you?" she managed to ask him as his mouth moved lower.

"I love it. It's terrific," he repeated quietly. "But in about five seconds I'm going to rip it right off your body, sweetheart. And I'm sure it wasn't cheap."

He lifted his head again and surveyed her, from her new hairstyle to the tips of her polished toes. He didn't have to say a word. No flowery compliment could ever convey the look of masculine approval and raw desire in his eyes. A look that stole her breath away and rocked her down to her soul.

Every doubt and question Maura had about her looks was instantly erased. Now she felt only a deep, sure sense that she was attractive to him. Practically irresistible, it seemed, with a special kind of allure she'd never really known she had before.

It was a strange new feeling for her. But when she once again caught the look of raw desire on Doug's face as he watched her unzip her dress, she had to admit it thrilled her.

With Doug's help, she unfastened the zipper at her back, and his large hands swiftly slid the dress off her body. Before the colorful pool of fabric had even hit the floor, he'd lifted her off her feet and tossed her on the bed. Then he pulled off his shirt and pants before dropping down beside her.

Seconds later her eyes closed as their mouths and bodies met in a deep, soulful kiss. While he had been the passionate aggressor this time, she felt a strange, new power over him.

A power purely feminine.

As Doug kissed and caressed her like a starving man sitting down to a feast, Maura had to admit she liked it.

She liked it a lot.

The next morning Maura woke up to full sunlight streaming through the bedroom windows. She quickly sensed that Doug's side of the bed was empty and she was shocked to see that she had slept until nearly ten. She got up and headed for the bathroom, amazed by her reflection. She'd forgotten all about the new hair-cut and hardly recognized herself as she brushed her teeth and washed her face.

In the kitchen Maura was greeted by the tantalizing scent of hot coffee and bacon. The table was set for breakfast, and Doug stood at the stove, cooking his signature dish—scrambled eggs.

"Gee, that coffee smells good," Maura said, head-ing straight for the pot with her empty mug. "I can't believe you let me sleep so late."

"Guess your day at the spa just wore you out," he teased her, glancing over one broad shoulder.

"Something wore me out," she replied with a slow smile over the edge of her mug. "I think it was the night after the spa, actually."

He turned and met her glance, the sexy gleam in his golden eyes unmistakable. She knew they were thinking the same thing, recalling the way they'd made love last night. And that with little encourage-ment there could be a repeat performance this morning. Maura's body reacted just thinking about it, but she tried not to show it.

"We never did get to that dinner reservation," he noted with a deep laugh, spooning some eggs into her dish and then his own.

"I don't think we ever had dinner," Maura realized. No wonder she was so hungry. "Hmm, this looks good."

She took a bite of eggs and put some jelly on a piece of toast. Doug sat down across from her, picked up a section of the newspaper and scanned the front page. Then after a moment or two he said, "What about taking a ride today? There's a wonderful old inn on a lake that I know of. I thought we could drive up there and hike around or maybe rent a rowboat."

"Sounds great," Maura replied around a mouthful of food. "I'd love to get out of the city. Should we pack a picnic?"

Doug smiled and picked up his coffee. "We can have lunch at the inn. You don't need to lift a finger today, Maura. I just want to see you relax."

He gave her a stern look over the top of his newspaper, and Maura felt a rebellious smile turning up the corners of her mouth.

"Yes, Doctor," she said with mock passivity.

"That's more like it," he teased back, snapping his newspaper as he turned the page.

While Doug scanned the headlines, Maura concentrated on her breakfast. She was pleased that he'd thought of spending the day this way with her. They certainly had a lot of boring things around the house they could do instead, including unpacking the rest of his belongings. This would be much more fun. More like a romantic date—the kind of plans you would make with someone you'd recently met and were happy just to be with them. Despite the passionate, physical intimacy they'd shared, she felt oddly excited, as if they were about to go out on a first date.

She and Doug had skipped all the usual trappings of a courtship, Maura realized, and had gone straight for domesticity, with its real-life pressures and unromantic routines. Maybe if they backtracked a little and spent time together, as they would today, or she surprised him with some candlelight dinners and even sexy lingerie, Doug would see her in a more romantic light—less as a friend he was helping out of a jam and more as a woman he could truly fall in love with.

No matter how many nights he spent making passionate love to her, Maura knew by now that it didn't mean he loved her. But she hoped in her heart that somehow she could make him fall in love with her and maybe this day was the start. It gave her hope.

The weather was perfect, and they drove with the top down. Maura loved the feeling of the warm sun on her skin. They didn't have much conversation as they drove, but it was a relaxing kind of quiet between them.

The inn was a rambling Victorian structure, built in the Queen Anne style, with turrets and gables and a wide shady porch that wrapped completely around. "What a beautiful place," Maura exclaimed as they drove up. "It's really fantastic. I love the colors," she added.

The lavender, purple, deep blue and hot pink that colored the building and intricate trim was a risky choice, she thought, but somehow it worked without looking overdone.

"I thought you would like this place." Doug looked pleased, she noticed, as if congratulating himself for predicting her reaction.

They picked up maps of walking trails and set out on their hike. Maura felt as if she could have walked all day, but Doug was concerned about her getting too tired. He'd brought along plenty of water and had her stop to drink every thirty seconds, it seemed to Maura.

"Doug, for goodness' sake. Pregnant women are supposed to exercise. It's good for the baby," she reminded him. "Please stop fussing over me."

She watched the play of emotions on his rugged features and could see him fighting to push back feelings of concern.

"I know all about your condition. I'm a doctor, remember? You're not used to anyone taking care of you, are you, Maura?"

His question was academic. They both knew the answer. "I've been on my own a long time, I guess," she admitted. She took a long sip of her water and turned her gaze toward the distant landscape.

"You'd better get used to it. I'm going to be around for a while."

Maura laughed and looked up at him, surprised by his strong tone. "Is that a threat or a promise?"

"It's a fact," he replied, meeting her eye.

Maura was the one to finally look away, taking another long drink. She forced herself to appear unfazed by their exchange, yet secretly felt cheered by his vow of commitment.

They came to a place in the trail where the walking was more difficult, the path steeper and covered with loose stones. Doug went ahead and gripped her hand, making sure she didn't lose her footing. Maura was surprised at first by his caution. They weren't exactly scaling the Rocky Mountains. But he was worried about the baby, she realized, and he was the type to get that protective male thing going big-time, she thought. Wasn't that a big part of his reason for marrying her in the first place?

After they'd hiked and rested in the cool shade by the lake, they went inside for lunch. As Maura had expected, the decor was elegant and elaborate and perfectly Victorian. Maura knew a little about antiques and the style of that era and was able to answer a few of Doug's questions.

"I can picture you in an old house someday, Maura. Something rambling and needing repairs," he added. "But with definite showplace potential. I bet you'd like that much better than a brand-new house, right?"

"A house? I hadn't really been thinking about moving, to tell you the truth," Maura admitted.

She felt surprised at his comment. She didn't think he imagined her in any specific kind of house. She'd never suspected he gave much thought to their future at all.

"I mean after the baby comes," he explained. "The apartment will be fine at first. But we'll need more room after a while. I thought we'd probably just move out of the city. It would be best for the baby, I think."

"Uh, yes. It probably would be," she agreed.

"We couldn't move too far out. Not right away, anyway," Doug added, then he named a few suburban areas he thought would work out for them. "I understand there are some great old houses in Norwood, too," he added.

It appeared that he'd been giving some thought to their future, Maura realized. She felt surprised but pleased.

"I've heard that, too," she replied. "And I do like old houses. Though they can be a lot of work. I think you probably have to be willing to do a good part of it yourself." She looked down at her menu. "You don't seem to have much spare time. And I'm not sure you'd like to spend it on a fixer-upper," she added with a small smile.

"Me? Are you kidding?" he insisted. "I could make a fortune doing that type of work if I ever decide to give up medicine," he insisted. "I worked on construction jobs all through college. Learned a lot, too."

"Really?" He'd never mentioned that before, but she could definitely picture him on a construction site, with a hard hat and bare, bronzed chest. The image was quite distracting.

"I'm definitely the handy type, Maura," he said with a sexy grin, "in case you haven't noticed."

Maura felt herself blush and lifted her menu a bit higher to hide her face. "I noticed," she replied blandly. Then she heard him laugh.

The waiter took their order, and they talked about other things. But very soon Doug's mind was back on the future again and willing Maura to go there with him.

"So, do you think you'll still want to work after the baby comes?" he asked.

"I'm not sure," Maura replied honestly. "I haven't thought about it much."

"You have time to think about it," Doug replied. He took a bite of his grilled trout. "You don't have to go back to work if you don't want to, Maura. We can afford to let you take a break from nursing for a while. Those first years pass quickly, they say. You might regret it if you don't stay home with the baby."

He was talking to her like a "real" husband now, Maura thought. It made her so emotional, her food fairly stuck in her throat. She put her fork down and took a sip of water, too moved to speak.

"What about our…agreement?" she finally dared to ask. He looked puzzled. "To see how we felt about the marriage after the baby comes."

"Oh…oh, of course." His expression turned from a warm, open look to something darker and far less revealing. She wondered what he was thinking but couldn't tell. "I'm just assuming that we'll both agree to stay together once the baby comes. But maybe I shouldn't. Maybe you're already having some doubts?"

"Me? No, not really," she said quietly. She looked down at the table, collecting her thoughts. She did have doubts. She didn't know how long she could stay with Doug, carrying on this marriage charade, knowing in her heart he didn't love her. Maybe it was time to tell him that. But when she glanced back up at him, she wondered if she'd been making a huge mistake. She already knew he didn't like being handed ultimatums, and if she tried to be honest with him about her feelings, it might sound as if she was pushing him into some kind of emotional corner. Fall in love with me or else. She certainly didn't think that would get her very far.

She stared at him and sighed. If only she could believe that he felt for her what she felt for him, that they were a couple truly in love, anticipating the birth of this baby. But he didn't. He would have told her by now.

"What is it, Maura? Have I said something to upset you?" he asked finally.

She shook her head. "No, not at all," she lied. "I guess it's just about overwhelming to talk about the future like this when I still have a long way to go with my pregnancy."

"Of course it is. I understand," Doug said. He covered her hand with his. "I didn't mean to... overwhelm you. I guess we'll just have to wait and see how you feel. How we both feel after the baby comes," he added in a cautious tone.

"Yes, I guess we will," she murmured.

Surprising her, Doug reached over and touched her hand. "You're not alone in this, Maura. That's the whole idea. I think that sometimes you forget that."

When he met her gaze, his smile was tender and caring and warmed her heart. It wasn't the confession of love she longed to hear...but it was something.

They ended the day, floating around the calm blue lake in a rowboat. Doug did the heavy work as Maura sat back, trailing her hand in the water like a lady of leisure. Sometimes they talked and sometimes they just enjoyed the tranquil atmosphere together. The sunset was stunning, signaling the end of their day.

They watched it sink behind the lush woods on the lake bank, holding hands but not saying a word.

As they drove back to the city, Maura thought back to the night Doug had proposed to her and remembered how dark the future had looked to her then. Today their talk about the days to come had made her a bit anxious. But maybe their future would work out as Doug had envisioned. That seemed too wonderful for her to even imagine.

Even if he didn't love her, if this day together was any clue, given time he might come to feel much more.

Given time, it seemed to Maura just then, anything was possible.

Six

Doug wasn't the only one who noticed Maura's look. Even co-workers and friends began to comment. "It's just something different about you," her friend Liza pointed out as they met for coffee and caught up on each other's lives. "I know it sounds silly, but it's like you just have this wonderful...glow."

Maura suddenly coughed into her steamed milk drink. A glow? Didn't people always say that about pregnant women?

"Must be the new makeup," Maura replied, hiding her reaction behind the large mug.

"More like the new husband," Liza observed. "Doug is a total babe. Even if he wasn't a Connelly, he'd be hot."

Maura blushed. "Thanks," she said quietly.

"It's so hard to meet anyone who's just plain decent, let alone a guy like Doug. You're so lucky, Maura,'' Liza added, clearly happy for her friend but envious, as well.

Lucky? It certainly must seem that way from the outside. Especially to Liza, Maura realized, who was so focused on getting married. Liza was her closest friend, and Maura had the sudden urge to confess everything—the secret circumstances of her marriage, her pregnancy...and the agonizing fact that she had fallen in love with Doug but he didn't love her.

But she stopped herself. For one thing, she'd promised Doug that they would keep their arrangement a secret and decide together when to tell everyone about the baby.

And for another, it was just too hard to admit even to her best friend. Maura was sure she'd break down and cry uncontrollably. Every day it got harder and harder to keep from confessing her love to him. In her heart she feared that such honesty would scare him and maybe even drive him away. He'd been hurt by his first marriage, and as Maura saw it, he didn't want to relive those messy, complicated emotions. He didn't want to feel so utterly dependent on someone else for his happiness. He'd made no pretense about it, either, she had to admit. Love was never part of their agreement.

Liza had started talking about her current relationship, and Maura turned her full attention back to her friend's conversation. It was far easier to listen to Liza's romantic dilemmas than think about her own.

Maura enjoyed visiting with Liza, but made sure she was home in plenty of time to cook dinner. It was one of the rare nights when she and Doug would be home together, and she wanted to make the evening special. Their afternoon in the country had convinced her that some courtship rituals might be just the thing she needed. Tonight was the perfect chance to move full speed ahead with her secret plan. She decided to make paella, one of her best dishes. She knew Doug liked it and she looked forward to surprising him.

She'd even bought fresh flowers and candles for the table and had taken out her best china. Maura was just about to shower and change when the phone rang. Thinking it was Doug, she picked it up on the first ring.

"Maura? Hi, it's me, Scott."

Shocked to hear Scott Walker's voice, she couldn't answer for a moment. She said hello and endured his small talk for a few moments before asking point-blank why he had called her.

"Oh, I don't know. Heard you got married. To my old pal, Doug, no less. I just wanted to wish you both good luck."

"You're kidding, right?" Maura was incredulous.

"Now, Maura, don't be like that," he urged in a tone that long ago had always soothed her. "I was just curious to find out how it was working out for you two. That's all."

"Your interest is touching, Scott," Maura replied with undisguised bitterness.

"I'm just concerned for you, honestly," he persisted. "I thought it all sounded pretty sudden. Especially considering your...special circumstances."

He knew that was his polite way of referring to her pregnancy. *Her* special circumstances. As if she managed to get pregnant all by herself.

"I knew you two were friends. Maybe I didn't realize how friendly," Scott added.

"Meaning what?" Maura challenged him.

"Meaning…well, you know what I mean. Maybe I'm not even the father of your baby, Maura. Maybe Doug Connelly is. Why else would he jump in and marry you like that? I think I have the right to know the truth," he added in an indignant tone, casting himself as the injured party.

Maura was so angry she couldn't see straight. She took a few deep, calming breaths, remembering that she had to think of the baby.

"The truth is, how was I so gullible to ever get involved with a man like you?" she returned in a ragged voice. "How dare you call me up and make such accusations. I never want to hear from you again in my life, Scott. Do you understand?"

"Now, Maura. You don't have to—"

But Scott's voice was cut off as Maura slammed down the phone.

When Doug walked in moments later, Maura was still sitting at the kitchen table trembling with anger and trying to compose herself.

"Maura, are you all right?" Doug rested a hand on her shoulder, gazing down at her with concern.

"I'm fine. I just had a phone call from Scott is all," she related.

"Walker? What was he calling you for?" Doug asked with an angry edge to his voice.

"He'd heard we'd gotten married and he wanted to wish us luck," Maura relayed with a bitter edge.

"Is that so?" Doug gazed at her quizzically. "That's all he had to say?"

"He did think it was sudden," she added. That was the truth, in part. Still she hesitated to relate the uglier details of the conversation.

Doug was silent for a moment, studying her. "How did you feel talking to him again?"

She shrugged. *Enraged* was a word that came to mind. But if she admitted that, the rest of the story was bound to come tumbling out.

"Mostly shocked that he called, I guess."

Doug crossed his arms over his chest. His face was a dark, unreadable mask. "Did he say something to upset you?"

Maura looked up at him, then away. She hated to lie to him, but the truth was too ugly to relate. She didn't want this to escalate and have Doug react by calling Scott back. She never wanted to have anything to do with Scott again.

"Like what?" she asked finally.

"Like…he had regrets about the way he'd treated you. Or he missed you and he wanted you back," Doug suggested, his tone low and objective, like a prosecuting attorney moving in on the witness.

Maura's eyes widened. She stood up and went over to the sink to pour herself a glass of water. "No, it was nothing like that. Nothing like that at all."

His gaze remained fixed on her. He didn't look convinced. His reaction puzzled her. What was he upset about? If she didn't know better, she'd think he was jealous.

Don't be silly, she told herself. A certain possessive streak had kicked in, perhaps. Combined with his deep disdain for Scott. But jealous? Not likely, Maura decided.

"Do you think you'll hear from him again?" Doug asked.

"Absolutely not. I told him very clearly not to call here anymore," she replied honestly.

Doug didn't reply, his mouth fixed in a hard straight line, his brows drawn together in a dark look. She wanted to move toward him, to put her arms around him and assure him that she had no feelings for Scott Walker other than anger and disdain. It's you I love, don't you know that by now, she wanted to say. But he seemed so distant, and she didn't have the courage to reach out to him.

Besides, Doug didn't love her, she reminded herself. How could he be insecure or even jealous? It was just her own wishful thinking, Maura realized.

Doug's schedule had changed and he needed to return to the hospital that night. Maura took the news easily, but saw her carefully laid romantic plans suddenly dissolve. They ate quickly and discussed unimportant matters. Though Doug kept complimenting her on the dinner, the atmosphere remained heavy and tense, the shadow of Scott Walker's call hovering over them.

"I'm sorry I have to rush through this great meal and take off again, Maura," Doug said as he prepared to go.

"That's okay, I understand." She did understand and tried not to sound too disappointed.

"Don't bother to wait up for me," he added. "I might be late."

Maura nodded. A lump had lodged in her throat, making it hard to speak. She felt sad and confused, as if something important had suddenly changed between them and she couldn't say why.

The apartment seemed silent and empty the instant she heard the front door close. Maura thought it was funny how before Doug had come along she'd never felt lonely when she'd been at home by herself. But now she wandered from room to room, as if missing some lost part of herself.

She blew out the candles and picked up the vase of flowers. The romantic trimmings seemed silly now, and she felt embarrassed by her hopeful plans. She showered and then got into bed with one of her thick what-every-expectant-mother-needs-to-know   books and soon fell asleep.

When Doug returned hours later, Maura roused, aware of him undressing in the dark and then slipping into bed beside her. She waited for him to reach for her, as he always did. But when he rolled over and seemed to fall asleep, she didn't have the courage to reach out to him, even though her arms ached to hold him near.

It was the end of a long hard day, a day of meetings and decisions and many people bringing all kinds of problems to his door. Grant Connelly flipped open a folder of documents that required his signature and reviewed the first on the pile. When his intercom buzzed, he reached over and answered it automatically.

"There's a visitor here for you, Mr. Connelly. Ms. Angie Donahue." His assistant's smooth, professional tone could not hide the hint of question. Charlotte Masters knew his daily schedule better than he did, and it rarely included unexpected visitors, unless it was Emma or one of the children.

But Angie Donahue, of all people.

Grant pulled off his reading glasses and tossed them on the desktop. What was she doing here? Maybe it was something to do with Seth, he thought with sudden concern.

But why not call? Why just pop in on him unannounced?

But that was Angie. Always assuming the world revolved around her and would indeed stop if she so much as snapped her fingers.

Grant reached over and pressed the intercom button to reply.

"Send her in," he said briskly. Might as well see what she had to say for herself after all these years. He had to admit, he was curious.

He smoothed back his hair with a careless gesture, straightened his tie and slipped his suit jacket on, just in time to hear a soft knock on the office door. "Come in, please," he called out.

Angie opened the door slowly and entered. He stood up and walked around his large desk to greet her.

"Hello, Grant. Aren't I terrible, popping in on you like this?" she asked with a girlish laugh as she offered her hand. "It's good of you to see me. I know you're always so horribly busy."

He took her hand lightly and shook it in both his own. "What a surprise. Goodness, it's been so long. You look great," he said. "You haven't changed a bit."

In many ways the easy compliment was true. Her

style had changed little since years ago, he noticed. She had never been shy about drawing attention to herself. Her platinum-blond hair and gold jewelry made a striking contrast with a formfitting red suit. She was still slender, and her sexy black heels added to her height so that her amber eyes were nearly staring directly into his own.

"Thank you, Grant. That's nice of you to say," Angie replied graciously. "You look wonderful, too." She lifted her eyes to meet his gaze with a look of pure feminine adoration that had once been so effective at melting his willpower.

Angie was one of those women who fought nobly to preserve their appearance. But the shine on her beauty-queen looks had diminished not without the help of plastic surgery and over the years, he noticed.

Angie settled herself gracefully on a long leather couch, and Grant sat nearby on an upholstered armchair.

"Believe it or not, I was having lunch with a friend at a restaurant just a block or two away and as I passed by the building on my way downtown again, I just stopped and said, hey, why not go up and see Grant?" she explained brightly. "Seth talks about you all the time, you know. And it's made me think of you. About the past, I mean," she added in a softer tone.

Grant forced a smile. He was hardly in the mood to go strolling down memory lane with Angie Donahue, and sincerely hoped that wasn't her agenda.

"Well, we can't go back in time, you know. We can only go forward," he said firmly. "I think it's good that you and Seth are back in touch."

"Oh, yes, it's been wonderful. You and Emma have done such a wonderful job raising him. He's so intelligent and successful. I was just…so proud. How can I ever thank you? I can't really, I know…"

She suddenly looked moved to tears, and Grant averted his gaze for a moment, not knowing what to say. But she'd always had that mercurial quality, he recalled, happy one moment, emotional the next. At first it had seemed so fascinating to him, so exciting. Until he realized that Angie was really quite calculating and theatrical, an actress in search of a stage.

"Yes, we're very proud of him," he said simply. "I know it's meant a lot to him to get to know you. It was good of you to get in touch. It couldn't have been easy," he added, giving her some credit for initiating the relationship.

"Thank you, Grant. That's kind of you to say…all things considered," Angie glanced up at him with wide amber eyes. Still casting those innocent, little-girl glances, even at her age, he noticed. "But I've had a lot of time to think about the past…the mistakes I've made. I could have been a better mother. I can see that now," she said very seriously. "I'm just grateful that he wants to have some relationship with me now, and I'm trying my best to make it up to him any way that I can." Angie met his gaze directly. "You know, I am sorry about the past. The way I treated Seth…and you, too, Grant. I know I can't go back and change any of it now, but I can tell you that I do have regrets."

Grant took a breath and sat back in his chair. This admission was so unlike the woman he'd always known, it was a moment before he could take it all in. Maybe she had changed. Maybe he'd been too cynical, too harsh on her.

"I don't really think about those days," he replied. "We both made our mistakes and I hold no bitterness toward you, believe me," he added honestly. "As for Seth, he appreciates your efforts toward making amends with him," Grant assured her. "We all do."

Angie looked thoughtful for a moment, then her perfectly drawn mouth formed a tentative smile. "Well, enough about me. How have you been?" she asked, suddenly changing the subject. "How's business?"

He replied in a pleasant, general manner, as he might to any stranger. Angie Donahue had once been his assistant, confidante, mistress and everything in between. Privy to his business dealings down to the last detail. How strange it seemed now to realize that they were once on such intimate terms, Grant reflected. Today he'd hardly feel comfortable disclosing even information that was public knowledge. She had long ago lost his trust, and it would take more than a few words of apology to regain it.

The intercom sounded and Grant excused himself to answer it. "I'm leaving now, Mr. Connelly," Charlotte informed him. "Is there anything you need before I go?"

"No, Charlotte. Thank you. Have a good evening," he replied.

"Thanks. Good night," Charlotte replied.

When Grant returned to Angie, she glanced at her watch and abruptly stood up.

"Oh, dear. Look at the time. I didn't mean to keep

you so long. You must need to be off, as well,'' she apologized.

''I have a nice pile of work to get through first,'' Grant said, glancing over at the thick report on his desk. ''And some calls to make. So I'll be here awhile yet.''

''Well, some things never change, I guess,'' she said with a smile. She picked up her purse and tucked it under her arm.

''Maybe,'' Grant agreed. ''It was good to see you, Angie,'' he said, holding out his hand. ''Glad you stopped by.''

She took his hand in both of hers and held it gently. ''I think you really mean that. So I'm glad I followed my hunch and surprised you.'' She opened the door and let herself out. ''See you sometime soon, okay? Let's not let another twenty years go by.''

''Yes, of course.'' He smiled, relieved to see her go. ''So long, Angie.''

The door closed and she was gone. Grant returned to his desk but felt too distracted to get back to work. What was that all about? he wondered. After twenty years and probably passing this building hundreds of times in her travels around the city, she suddenly had the impulse to stop and say hello?

He shook his head and put his reading glasses on again. Maybe it was inspired by seeing Seth and thinking about the past. Since Seth had a relationship with her again, they'd be bound to run into each other at some point, Grant speculated, so maybe it was better to break the ice this way, in private.

Still, he had the niggling feeling that she'd been

after more. That there was some other purpose to her coming here. Though what it was he couldn't say.

He would have to tell Emma about this. She was always very savvy about unraveling a person's motives. He was sure she'd have some interesting insight into Angie's hidden agenda.

In the outer office, Angie was delighted to find herself completely alone. She noticed an extension light illuminated on Charlotte's phone. Grant was busy with his phone calls. She waited just a beat, then smoothly moved behind Charlotte's desk and turned on the computer. In some distant part of her mind she wondered what she would tell Grant if he suddenly came out and caught her here. But he wouldn't, she coached herself as she opened her purse and removed a computer diskette. She would be done with her nasty little deed in a matter of seconds.

She inserted the diskette into the computer and swiftly struck the appropriate keys, then watched the message as the files from her disk transferred onto the hard drive of Charlotte's computer. In a matter of sinister seconds her handiwork was done.

Angie removed her diskette and shut down the computer. Then she removed a small white business card from her purse and left it squarely in the center of Charlotte's neat desk.

Angie snapped her purse closed and swiftly left Charlotte's office. The rest of the floor seemed empty, as well, with the lights off in every office door as she passed by. Her stiletto heels clicking noisily in the empty corridor as she headed for the elevators, Angie felt elated with the success of her visit.

She hadn't been back in here in over twenty years, but her little surprise visit had certainly been a productive one. When Charlotte turned on her computer tomorrow morning, before you could say Connelly Corporation, the virus on the hard drive would spread through the network of computers in the entire company in a matter of seconds. It would contaminate everything, effecting a gigantic crash of the entire system.

Angie stepped into the elevator and felt a gleeful thrill as she punched the button for the lobby. Charlotte would at first be baffled. Then she would remember the anonymous call she'd received last week, informing her that sometime soon the system would crash and she'd find a business card on her desk, with the name of some outside computer technicians. All she had to do to correct the problem was call in the outside experts. She had been told that everything would be easily fixed if she hired the right people to do the job.

But if she didn't cooperate, Grant Connelly and everyone else in the company would soon learn about her brother, Brad, who was currently serving time in Deer Lodge Prison for drug possession and trafficking. Not only would that be embarrassing for Charlotte, who'd gone to great lengths to hide her truth, but it might even cost her her job.

Angie had only met the young woman briefly, but she had a feeling Charlotte would comply. What choice did she have? Angie sighed and slipped on her sunglasses as she strolled through the lobby.

What choice do any of us have, when you get right down to it? she wondered. Sometimes she felt as if her life had been scripted down to each precious minute and she had no choice at all in the paths she'd followed or the mistakes she'd made. But even if it could be different for her, even at this late date, she knew in her heart she didn't really want to change. She was far too comfortable with things just as they were.

Seven

As the car sped along the highway toward the Connelly country home at Lake Geneva, Maura hoped the change of scenery would help dispel the tension that had come between her and Doug these past few days. She'd even worked up the courage to ask him if something was wrong. But he'd shrugged off her inquiry with some mumbled, vague reply. Then he'd hardly said a word to her or even met her eye as they'd packed and started the trip to his parents' cottage.

Maybe he was just nervous about tonight, Maura speculated. She definitely was. The party to celebrate their marriage would officially start sometime during the late afternoon, but Grant and Emma had urged them to arrive a bit earlier. Emma said they had a surprise waiting, which both Maura and Doug expected to be a wedding gift that her in-laws wanted to give in private. Doug was eager to get to the lake, hoping for a sail on one of Grant's boats. Since Maura had been having a lot of morning sickness lately— and not just in the morning—she thought she'd skip the ride. But a refreshing plunge in the lake might be nice.

At other times like these, Doug had always had a way of making her feel better about her shyness. But he seemed so distracted right now she didn't feel comfortable confiding in him. In fact, over the past few days, she'd hardly felt comfortable talking to him at all. And he seemed to feel the same about her. They hadn't made love or even touched each other.

Maura wasn't sure what had happened exactly. There had been no argument or even a quiet disagreement. But ever since Wednesday night, when her plans for a romantic dinner had not worked out, the atmosphere between them had grown strained. She wondered if Doug was suddenly getting nervous about having married her.

Maybe her scheme to romance him had been too transparent and appeared too desperate. There was nothing that would cool a man's interest sooner. Maybe he was intentionally pulling away from her now, just to make it clear that he wasn't about to change the terms of their deal. He'd had enough romance with his first wife. He wasn't interested in falling in love.

If that wasn't the cause of his distant attitude toward her, what was? It seemed so ironic that here they were about to have a huge party thrown in honor of their marriage and they were barely speaking to each

would be an excellent solution. Except that I've forgotten to bring the number, and I doubt that it's listed.''

''Oh…'' Maura sat back in her seat again, staring down at the nearly indecipherable marks Doug was calling directions. ''That's not so good.''

Doug seemed amused at her distress. ''Trust me, Maura. You may be feeling a little lost right now but we'll find our way.''

Maura held his gaze for a moment, feeling as if he was speaking to her about much more than the route to his parents' vacation house.

''I hope so,'' she replied. ''I really do.''

Doug looked back at the road. He reached over and covered her hands with his. The simple gesture held more intimacy and affection than he had shown her in days, and Maura soaked up his touch.

Somehow they did find the house, and without too many wrong turns, Maura noticed. A long gravel road led down to the house, which was close to the lakeshore. The property looked vast to Maura, a large part of it wooded. But as they approached the house, she spotted tennis courts, a pool and, in the distance, the stables and riding ring.

Emma and Grant were outdoors and came to the car to meet them. Emma gave Maura a big hug while simultaneously admiring her outfit, one that Maura had bought on the recent shopping trip.

Doug was eager to take a tour of the grounds with Grant to the lake, but Emma insisted that they both come inside first. ''Just for a minute,'' she urged. ''I just want to give you your surprise.''

Doug glanced at Maura. How could they refuse?

"Of course," he said graciously, touching Maura lightly at the small of her back as they walked up the path to the lake house.

The "cottage," as Grant and Emma called it, was stunning, and Maura paused for a moment on the path to admire the strong, clean lines of its design. The original cottage had been designed by Frank Lloyd Wright, Grant explained, but over the years they'd needed to expand and had made some changes. Floor to ceiling windows in a wide open great room framed a view of the dark blue lake. The Mission-style furnishings looked casual and relaxed, Maura noticed, yet were no doubt the best money could buy.

While Maura and Doug admired the house and took in the view, Emma disappeared for a moment into an adjoining room. She returned moments later and stood in the doorway. "Maura and Doug, here's your surprise," she announced happily. "Tobias and Miss Lilly. When they heard you eloped I couldn't keep them away. They've come up from Palm Springs for the party."

Maura recognized the names instantly. They were Doug's grandparents, Grant's parents. Doug had only met them once, and briefly at a party to welcome him and Chance into the family. Tobias had a stout but solid build and bore a strong facial resemblance to Grant. Miss Lilly was quite attractive with smooth clear skin that was practically wrinkle free and a soft halo of pure white hair.

"Doug, how nice to see you again," Tobias said as he heartily shook Doug's hand.

"Hello, grandson," Lilly said simply. "Goodness,

I can't get over how handsome you are!'' She got up on tiptoe and pulled Doug close for kiss on the cheek.

Doug looked pleased, Maura thought. Grant and Emma stood aside, looking on at the reunion without interrupting.

''Let me introduce you to my wife,'' Doug said. ''Tobias, Lilly, this is Maura.''

He put his arm around Maura and drew her close, and Maura suddenly felt connected to him again, as if they were a real couple.

Suddenly Emma announced that lunch was served on the patio, and everyone moved out through the glass doors. As they took their places around the large round table, Maura realized that she was very grateful for the distraction that Tobias and Lilly provided. Now Doug would be the center of attention for a while and she was let off the hook.

The conversation around the table was lively, with Doug's grandparents peppering their grandson with questions. Maura felt her shyness slip away and found it easier than she expected to talk about herself and join in.

Once lunch was cleared away, the men went off to walk the grounds and see about taking the sailboat out for a quick spin. Emma ran off to see to some last-minute details about the party, and Miss Lilly retired to her room for a nap.

Maura was grateful for the time alone. She changed into her bathing suit and walked down to the lake. The swimming and sun felt wonderful, but soon left her feeling too tired to even walk back to her room. But she did, immediately falling across the bed and going to sleep.

Her dreams were vivid—mostly about Doug. She held a baby in her arms and handed it over to him. The look of pure joy on his face was unmistakable as he lifted the child toward the sky. Then he turned toward Maura and kissed her deeply on the mouth. Maura felt herself kissing him back, cupping his cheek with her hand. She inhaled the scent of his warm skin, his hair. It felt so real—too real—and she opened her eyes to find Doug's face close to hers in the darkened room.

"Oh, it's you. You were kissing me," she said groggily.

"Yes, I did. Couldn't resist," he confessed, stroking her hair with his hand.

"I was having a dream." She sat up and pushed back her hair with her hand.

He sat up, too, moving away from her. "About your husband, I hope," he said lightly. Then added, "Wait. You don't have to answer that."

She watched him as he got up from the bed and pulled his shirt over his head. He had such a magnificent body—a sculpted, muscular chest and wide shoulders and narrow waist—it was hard to keep her mind on anything else. She wished they could make love right now, but knew they didn't have enough time before the party.

"Don't be silly. Of course it was about you," she replied with a nervous laugh.

"You can dream about whoever you like, Maura." He slung a towel around his neck and turned to go into the bathroom. "You don't owe me any explanations."

Maura felt taken aback. She didn't know what he

was driving at and felt unable to answer. He closed the door to the bathroom, and she heard the shower run. Glancing at the clock, she saw that it was quite late. The guests would be arriving soon and she wasn't anywhere near ready.

She would have to ask Doug later what he meant by his cryptic remark. Now it was time to play the happy newlyweds. This time for their biggest audience ever. Maura hoped she was up to the challenge.

Doug gripped her hand as they walked through the house and out to the patio. Most of the guests had already arrived, and everyone turned to greet Doug and meet Maura as they slowly made their way through the crowd.

In between introductions Maura gazed around in amazement at the way the outdoor area behind the cottage had been transformed for the gathering, with small white lights in the trees and glittering candles and flowers everywhere.

As waiters passed around trays of delicious-looking hors d'oeuvres and drinks, soft sounds of jazz from a trio of musicians set the perfect mood. A short distance from the deck, several large barbecues stood end to end, manned by chefs in tall white hats and red aprons. Smoke rose in thick plumes, carrying the appetizing scents of ribs, steaks and chicken. Maura was suddenly starving and plucked a huge shrimp canapé from a passing tray.

"If this is what your folks call a casual barbecue, I'd hate to see a really formal affair," Maura whispered to Doug at a rare free moment.

"Emma is used to doing things on a royal scale,"

he whispered back with a smile. "It's just the way she was raised, you might say."

"Please don't misunderstand," Maura added hastily, "I think it's lovely. I can't believe she went to all this trouble. I feel a little guilty actually, as if I don't quite deserve such treatment."

Doug's expression turned suddenly serious. He met her gaze, a questioning light flashing in his amber eyes. "Nonsense, you're my wife. Of course you do. Why would you say that?"

Maybe because this isn't a real marriage, she wanted to say. Because I love you and you don't feel the same about me.

Instead she shrugged and looked away. "I'm just not used to the deluxe treatment, I guess."

Doug did not reply, his expression brooding and unreadable. She wondered again what she had said or done to cause him to withdraw this way. Or was it really his own doubts and regrets at his impulsive proposal finally kicking in?

"There they are. The guests of honor." A tall handsome man, the image of Doug, stepped up and heartily shook Doug's hand, at the same time slapping him on the shoulder. "Where have you been? We've been looking all over for you."

Maura knew this had to be Doug's twin brother, Chance, who was a Navy SEAL. She had already met the beautiful woman who stood beside him, his fiancée, Jennifer.

Doug looked shocked at first, then his expression quickly changed to pure happiness as he first shook his brother's hand, then gave him a quick hug. "What are you doing here? I thought you were away."

"I got a short leave at the last minute. Thought I'd surprise you, Doc. Looks like it worked," Chance dryly observed before he turned to Maura with a wide smile. "Aren't you going to introduce me to your gorgeous wife?"

Doug made the proper introductions, exchanging a few brotherly barbs with Chance. Maura liked her new brother-in-law instantly and could quickly see that though the two men were physically identical, their personalities were just about opposite. Chance was charming, outgoing, even a bit brash—a distinct contrast to Doug's intense and sometimes brooding personality.

Chance and Doug had a lot to catch up on, and while they drifted off to fetch some drinks, Maura sat at a small table with Jennifer. She was glad to see Jennifer again. Although they'd only met once before, Maura had a feeling they could become close friends—if her marriage to Doug lasted that long.

"The dress looks fantastic. I'm so glad you kept it," Jennifer said, taking another look at the designer creation Maura had chosen during her outing with the Connelly women. "I bet Doug loved it," she added with a sly smile.

"Uh, yes, he did," Maura admitted. She could feel her cheeks growing warm as she recalled Doug's ravenous reaction. Though he'd hardly seemed to notice the outfit tonight, she reflected.

"Chance was so happy to make it here tonight," Jennifer confided. "He idolizes Doug, you know."

"Doug feels the same about Chance. I'm glad to have finally met this mysterious superbrother. He's described him as something between a superhero and James Bond,'' she added.

Jennifer's smile widened. "He's all that and more,'' she admitted with a smile. ''So how's married life? It seems to be agreeing with you so far.''

''So far,'' Maura replied, feeling a little tug at her conscience for the white lie.

''And how are you feeling?'' Jennifer's tone was casual, but Maura could tell by a certain light in her eyes that she knew about the pregnancy.

''Fine.'' Maura shrugged, pretending not to take the hint. ''A little tired from work, I suppose. It's nice to have a break in a place like this.''

''Well, don't overdo,'' Jennifer advised. ''I mean, in your condition.''

Maura felt angry at Doug for giving away their secret, even if it was to his brother. If Chance and Jennifer knew she was pregnant, how many other people here knew, as well?

''Oh, dear. I'm sorry.'' Jennifer leaned over and touched Maura's arm. ''I wasn't supposed to let you know that I know. I promised Chance a million times over that I wouldn't.'' She shook her head regretfully, looking embarrassed, and Maura had to forgive her.

''It's all right. I guess Doug really wanted to tell his brother the news. It's understandable,'' Maura said.

''Well, they are very close. And he's so happy, Maura. You have no idea. Especially since his first marriage broke up because his ex-wife didn't want children. Chance says that Doug has wanted a baby for so long,'' she added. ''This is really a dream come true for him.''

His wife didn't want children? That was why they'd broken up? If this was really true, then it all made sense. Doug had only married her for the baby. He didn't care for her at all, not in the way that really counted.

He'd never love her the way she loved him. He wanted to be a father, and she was a convenient mother-to-be. It was his dream come true—and her heartbreaking nightmare.

Maura felt stunned. She could barely breathe for a moment, and Jennifer's voice seemed to come from far away. She touched her hand to her forehead, feeling light-headed.

"Maura, are you okay?" Jennifer asked with concern. "You look so pale. Can I get something for you?"

"I'm okay. Really." Maura sat up again and tried to smile. She struggled to gain control of her feelings. She was in the middle of a party in her honor. She couldn't think about this now, couldn't face it.

Just then Doug and Chance appeared. "Maura isn't feeling that well," Jennifer reported. "I was just coming to find you."

Maura looked up to meet Doug's gaze. He was already taking her in with a sweeping look of concern. As Doug sat down beside her, she noticed that Chance and Jennifer politely drifted away, leaving them alone.

"Do you feel dizzy?" he asked. "Maybe your blood sugar dropped and you need something to eat," he suggested in a knowledgeable tone.

"Yes, that must be it," Maura agreed. She took a sip of the cold drink he offered and avoided his gaze.

"You didn't fall or anything did you?" Doug asked suddenly.

At first Maura was touched by his concern, then instantly felt resentful. He didn't really care about her, it was all about the baby. That was what had motivated his every action from the first. Only, she'd been too blinded by love to see the plain truth.

"No, I didn't fall," she replied a bit sharply. She stood up, despite the lingering unsteady feeling. "Let's get something to eat. I'm starved."

Doug placed his hand on her shoulder. "Wait here. I'll get it for you."

She had an impulse to shrug off his protective touch and refuse to be waited on. But she didn't. She acquiesced and sat down with a sigh while Doug disappeared into the crowd.

Her appetite suddenly disappeared as every considerate, caring gesture of his returned to mock her. This man didn't care about her, only the life growing inside of her. As if she were some prize broodmare in the Connelly stable!

The situation was intolerable. Maura thought she was going to burst into tears. But she couldn't embarrass the Connellys that way. They'd gone to so much trouble and expense. She had to keep up a good front, at least until she and Doug were alone and she could confront him. Maybe she was getting upset over nothing. Maybe Jennifer hadn't gotten the story straight. There was always that possibility to consider, Maura realized. The way to discover the truth was to ask Doug straight out. That was what she had to do.

While Maura sat waiting for Doug to return, Chance passed by again and began to chat. He took a seat to keep her company, and they were soon joined by Grant. Grant then introduced her to his son, Rafe, who sat down as well.

When Doug returned with a plate of food in each hand and found Maura sitting with the three men, he paused, his mouth twisting into a grin.

"Well, if isn't Scarlett O'Hara at the Twelve Oaks barbecue," he observed dryly. "I've brought you your dinner, Miss Scarlett. That at least rates a seat, don't you think?"

Everyone turned to look at him. Chance laughed out loud.

"Your wife is very charming," Rafe said, congratulating his stepbrother. "You're a lucky man," he added with a distinctly male grin.

"Thank you. I think so," Doug said quite definitely. He cast a quick glance in Maura's direction, but she avoided his gaze.

While Maura ate her dinner, Grant told Rafe about a major computer crash at Connelly Corporation. Rafe, it seemed, was a systems analyst and computer security expert in great demand, traveling around the country and the world to his top-level clients.

Maura thought she'd seldom seen anyone who looked less like a computer nerd in her life. With his easy smile, tanned skin and toned body, he looked more like an athlete than a desk jockey.

When his father finished talking, Rafe frowned. "I wish I could help. My schedule—"

Grant waved the apology aside. "I know, I know. You're booked solid. Phoenix, right?"

Rafe nodded, still frowning. "I'll be there at least

three months, maybe longer. Have your techs been able to get the system back up?''

"We called in some outside people—Broderton's Computing. Charlotte recommended them, and they seemed to be very good. We may want to use them again. They had things up and running again by the end of the day.''

"Broderton…" Rafe shook his head. "I'm not familiar with the company. What did they think caused the crash?''

"Some kind of virus. They said it probably arrived through e-mail.'' Grant frowned and added thoughtfully, "I'm no computer expert, but the whole episode seemed very odd. Our employees know better than to open e-mail attachments from outside the company. We send out reminders quite often. And we've got antivirus software.''

Rafe grinned. "It doesn't matter how often you tell some people not to open attachments—they do it, anyway. And I've been telling you for two years that your entire system needs to be updated.''

"I suppose.'' Grant took a sip of his drink and swirled the ice in his glass. "When you get back from Phoenix, we'll talk about you working Connelly Corporation into your schedule.''

"That's what you always say.''

"No, this time I mean it. That episode put a real scare in me.''

"If you're serious, you'd better have Charlotte call my secretarial service in the morning to get you scheduled. I'm booked pretty solid but I think I could work you in after Christmas.''

"Maybe I should just go with Broderton,'' Grant

said dryly. "They seem eager enough for my business that they wouldn't consider a trip to Cozumel more important than getting my system updated. You do still plan to spend a couple of weeks there, I heard."

Rafe grinned. "You know what they say about all work and no play. After Phoenix I'm going to deserve some play time. If you're in a hurry, though, let me check out this Broderton outfit— Wait, there's just the person we need to talk to." He raised his voice. "Hey, Charlie, come here a minute."

An attractive young woman with sleek, strawberry-blond hair was passing by. She stopped, frowned, then came over to their table. "You bellowed?" she said politely.

Rafe chuckled. Grant introduced the young woman to Maura—she was his assistant, Charlotte Masters. She had an interesting face, Maura thought. A little too strong for conventional prettiness, but very attractive.

Rafe seemed to think so, too, from the way he was looking at her. "What do you know about this outfit you called to fix the computers, Charlie? Could Broderton handle a system upgrade, or should my father wait until he gets the best?" He grinned. "Meaning me, of course."

"Broderton?" Her glance darted between Rafe and his father. "I don't know much about them, actually. They were recommended, but—but I don't think I'd use them for something that major." She let out a quick breath, as if she'd crossed some hurdle. "No, I wouldn't recommend them."

Rafe's smile faded and he studied her intently. "What's wrong?"

"What do you mean?"

"You didn't make any attempt to squash my ego just now, and you didn't complain when I called you Charlie. Something must be wrong."

"Oh." Her smile came and went too quickly. "As a matter of fact, I'm not feeling well. I was just going to find Emma and apologize for leaving early."

Grant was immediately concerned. He wouldn't hear of Charlotte driving herself home if she was ill. Rafe, Maura noticed, was quick to volunteer for that chore. Charlotte protested, but when two Connelly males decided to protect a woman, she got protected whether she liked it or not.

The rest of the party passed quickly. Maura was distracted from her worries by the constant conversation and socializing. After dinner Chance got up and made a warm, humorous and touching toast to his brother. Emma and Grant spoke, as well, welcoming Maura into the family with simple, sincere words that made tears come to her eyes. Ever since she'd lost her parents, and her home had been torn apart, Maura had longed to feel part of a family again. Now, after so long, she truly felt welcomed, even loved by these marvelous Connellys.

If only this could last forever, Maura wished. But as she glanced at Doug's strong profile beside her, she felt a dark note of dread in her heart. It wouldn't last. Not now. Not after the bitter truth she'd learned tonight.

When the party ended much later that night, she went up to bed, while Doug lingered, talking to his brother and other stepsiblings. Maura didn't want to seem rude, but she was thoroughly wiped out and fell asleep the moment her head hit the pillow.

The next morning she was awakened by the shrill ring of Doug's cell phone. He picked it up and groggily answered it, his head barely lifted from the pillow. Maura didn't have to ask to figure out the situation. He was needed at the hospital and had to leave right away.

"Shall I come with you? I just need five minutes," Maura promised as she started to get out of bed.

"No, you stay," Doug replied firmly. "Get some more sleep." He pulled on his pants and a clean shirt, then sat near her on the bed as he put on his shoes. "Grant and Emma will give you a ride back to the city. Or maybe Rafe. I think he stayed over last night, too."

"Don't worry. I'll get back all right. Don't bother to pack your things now. I'll take them with me," she offered.

He glanced at her and rested his hand on her hip. "Thanks." He paused and gazed deeply into her eyes. She sensed him leaning toward her and opened her mouth slightly, anticipating his kiss. But then he took a deep breath and turned away.

"Okay, then, I'd better get going." He stood up and grabbed his phone, wallet and keys off the night table. "See you back at home," he added as he headed for the door.

"Yes, see you later," Maura echoed dully.

She felt tears spring to her eyes, but wasn't sure why. She was suddenly grateful that it was barely dawn and the room was so dimly lit he couldn't see her parting reaction.

Eight

Over the next few days Maura tried many times to confront Doug but their schedules were not in synch. She could never quite find the right moment. Or just as she'd summon up her courage to speak to him, they would be interrupted by a call from the hospital or his office.

The tension she'd noticed before the party was now even more intense, since it wasn't just coming from Doug but from her corner, as well. Maura felt totally distracted and worn-out. She wasn't sleeping well and was hardly able to eat. She had to force herself to concentrate at work, and often asked other nurses to double-check her work. She knew she couldn't go on much longer this way, and by Friday morning she had resolved to finally have it out with him.

As Maura stood at the medication counter counting

out pills on Friday afternoon, she was so distracted by her worries she knocked over a full cart of medication. Pills went flying in all directions. Maura looked down at the mess in dismay, feeling so overwhelmed she thought she might burst into tears. She was so emotional lately. She knew it was only her hormones, but it was hard to handle the ups and downs.

Just as Maura bent over and started cleaning up the mess, her supervisor walked past and found her. "Lord, what's happened here?" Gloria exclaimed.

"Just a little clumsy today," Maura replied, coming to her feet.

Gloria looked long and hard into her eyes. "You haven't been yourself for weeks now, Maura. I know it isn't just honeymooning," she said. "I say you're pregnant. Tell the truth now."

"How did you know?" Maura asked in shock.

"I have four kids, remember? Besides, I can just see it in those pretty green eyes."

Maura had to smile at that unscientific pronouncement. "No, you can't. But that's besides the point."

"The point is you look beat and your shift is over in less than an hour so I want you out of here. I don't need any clumsy pregnant ladies messing the place up," Gloria insisted as she gently pushed Maura out to the corridor. "Now you go home and have that handsome husband give you a foot rub or something."

Little did Gloria realize she was sending Maura home to face more problems, not saving her from them. But Maura took her orders without argument, packed up her things and headed home.

She quickly changed out of her uniform and took a shower. As she stood in the bedroom, putting on her clothes, she heard Doug's key in the lock.

He swung open the door and called out to her. "Maura? Where are you?"

"Back here," she replied, wondering at the note of alarm in his voice. He walked back to the bedroom and stared at her. "Are you all right? I came up to your floor, and somebody told me Gloria sent you home early."

Maura took a deep breath. Once again his concern for her well-being struck a raw nerve. She swallowed hard, fighting back harsh words. "I knocked over some meds, and Gloria guessed that I'm pregnant. Nothing to worry about," she said evenly.

He walked closer to her and cupped her cheek in his hand. "Maybe you should rest."

Maura relished his touch for an instant, then abruptly pulled away. Suddenly it struck her how this conversation was almost an exact replay of the night he'd surprised her here and ended up proposing marriage.

If only she'd known then what she knew now, Maura thought.

"What is it?" Doug touched her shoulder, urging her to turn around again and face him.

"You worry about me too much," she said sharply, with her back still turned toward him. "Or maybe it's not me really…it's just the baby."

When she turned to face him, his expression was shocked, his eyes narrowed as he stared at her with a questioning look.

"Of course I'm worried about the baby. You're not

other. And definitely not in love. At least, Doug was not in love with her, she corrected. Although the lust factor was certainly strong enough to rival any new-lywed pair.

But Maura now knew better than to mistake a man's sexual appetite for emotional involvement. Could she ever resolve herself to it, she wondered. Loving a man who didn't love her? Living with a man who didn't love her? She didn't think she could. They had not even been married for a month, and already the burden was wearing on her.

She shifted in her seat and sighed aloud without realizing it. Doug turned to her. "Are you okay?" he asked quietly. "Would you like me to make a stop?"

She met his gaze, then looked out the window again. "I'm fine. How much longer is the ride?"

"We should be there in another half hour. Here, why don't you read these directions to me," he suggested, handing her a scrap of paper.

Maura scanned the sheet of directions. "I can see why you went into medicine," she said dryly. "Your handwriting is totally illegible. Is that a five or an *S?*" she asked, pointing out a scribbled word.

He glanced at the paper for a second, then looked back at the road. "I think it's a three with the top part squashed," he offered. "But I'm not totally certain."

She could see he was trying hard not to smile, and that made her smile, too. She took the paper back and stared at the indecipherable marks once more. "Well, no big deal. We have the cell phone. If we can't find our way, we can call."

He glanced at her, then back at the road. "That

even through the first trimester yet. You're still at high risk for a miscarriage,'' he reminded her, sounding very much like a physician, she thought.

''And what then, Doug?'' she challenged him. ''Would the deal be off?''

''The deal? What are you talking about, Maura? What deal?'' He stood with his hands on his hips, his brow knitted in a frown, his fine mouth a grim, hard line.

''The deal we made when we agreed to get married. You marry me, give my child a name, I in turn produce one baby. That's really the only reason you married me, isn't it? So you could have a baby.'' Her voice was thick with emotion, and she hated the sound of her own accusatory tone.

She saw him flinch, his face turning ashen at the sound of her words. She felt awful striking out at him like this, but she had to know the truth.

''I'd never deny that I like the idea of having a family. But I married you so that I could help you. Because you didn't deserve to be treated the way Scott treated you…even though you're probably still in love with him,'' he added in a burst of anger.

''In love with Scott? Don't be ridiculous,'' she scoffed. ''Now you're just trying to change the subject. I know why your first marriage broke up, Doug. Because you wanted to have a child and your wife refused. Isn't that the real truth?''

''Who told you that?'' His rough, low voice was barely above a whisper. He moved closer, his dark expression frightening to behold.

Maura instinctively took a step back, suddenly regretting she'd ever started this confrontation. But they had to get to the end of it, however painful the journey.

"It doesn't matter who," she replied, rallying her nerve. "It's true, isn't it?" she persisted, looking directly into his eyes. "You want a baby and there I was, ready to provide one for you, no questions asked."

Doug looked about to speak, then paused. She saw him take a deep breath, as if consciously trying to calm himself. Finally he said, "Look, I won't deny that I love children and have always wanted to be a father. I want this baby—and more children, too, if possible. But that's not the only reason I married you, Maura. And now that we've been together, I realize that there were other reasons I came to you that night when I proposed." He came closer and took her hands in his shoulders. "Listen," he began, "let's not ruin everything over some gossip, some misunderstanding…"

His words trailed off and he stared into her eyes, looking overwhelmed with feeling. Was he about to say that he loved her? Maura wished with all her heart that he would. It seemed the only way to save things between them now.

Finally, gripping her shoulders a bit tighter, he said, "It's not just the baby, Maura. I know this is right between us. I know it's good."

Maura felt the tears well up in her eyes. He hadn't said the words. He didn't love her. Feelings of heartbreaking disappointment mingled with her deep love for him. A love that would never be returned.

Unable to hold back her tears any longer, Maura pulled away, though his touch urged her to come into his arms. She turned from him, not wanting him to see the crushing disappointment in her eyes. She didn't want him to see how much she loved him.

"You may be perfectly satisfied by the arrangement, Doug. But I'm sorry," she said finally, "it's just not enough for me."

Doug looked stunned at her words. "What do you mean? What are you saying?"

She took a deep breath and whisked away her tears with her fingertips. "Our marriage...it isn't working out for me."

"But we've barely been together a month," he replied. "I thought we'd give this a chance at least until the baby was born."

The baby again. Maura thought she was about to scream.

"I know that's what I said," she replied, willing her voice to be slow and calm, "but I was wrong. I can't stay with you that long. I—" She started to say more, then stopped herself.

I didn't realize how hard it would be to live with you, knowing you only married me for the baby. Knowing that I love you so much and you can't seem to fall in love with me.

The unspoken words echoed in her mind as she stared at Doug's stunned expression.

"You can't do this," he said suddenly, coming toward her again. "I won't let you leave," he insisted with dark intensity.

Maura didn't know what to say. His reaction was some proof of his feelings for her, she supposed. But they were only feelings of possession or propriety.

Maybe he dreaded the embarrassment if she left him now.

Then, just as she was about to reply, the shrill sound of his cell phone cut through the silence.

"Blast!" Doug cursed as he pulled out the phone and answered the call. His words were curt and harsh to the caller. A few seconds later he snapped the phone closed and looked up at her, his expression grim.

"They just brought Jill Dixon back," he reported, mentioning a five-year-old patient who'd just had angioplasty during the week and had gone home yesterday. "The artery collapsed. They're prepping her for surgery."

Maura felt icy chills along her spine. She sent up a silent prayer that the child would survive and recover. Her own problems suddenly seemed small potatoes in comparison.

"Go," she told Doug. "You've got to get over there."

He nodded but didn't move. He stared at her, looking totally torn.

"Just promise me you won't do anything until I get back," he urged. "We can work this out. I know we can."

Maura didn't reply for a long moment.

"All right, I promise. Just go," she said finally. She knew in her heart that she was lying to him. But it was critical that he left for the hospital and worked on Jill Dixon with his mind as clear as possible.

After pausing to take her in with one long, sweeping look, Doug turned and stalked out of the room. She heard the door close and exhaled a long, pent up sigh. Then she sat down on the bed and dropped her head in her hands. She felt like crying her heart out, but knew she couldn't spare the time.

With effort, she rose and pulled an overnight bag out of her closet, then automatically packed some clothes and other essentials. She'd return for the rest later.

When she got outside to the street, the light rain of the early evening was falling heavier. She hardly noticed as she walked to her car, tossed in her suitcase and slipped behind the wheel.

It seemed a bit extreme and dramatic, even under the circumstances, to leave her own apartment, Maura thought as she drove away. But it was the only way. She'd have a hard time persuading Doug to move out. She had to be the one to go. She'd find a hotel for the weekend, she speculated, then maybe arrange for some time off to visit with her sister.

She needed to put some distance between herself and Doug, or else this would never work. She knew that if she gave Doug half a chance and five more minutes of her time, he'd persuade her to put her doubts aside and give their marriage another try.

She switched the windshield wipers to a higher setting, the steady rhythm marking time in her wandering thoughts. There was so much good in their relationship—their connection, their rapport, the respect and understanding they felt for each other. Not to mention the fantastic lovemaking.

She would never deny that there was a solid foundation of feeling here. But if he didn't love her it just wasn't good enough. If he loved her he would have told her by now. Clearly, he didn't want her to go and he knew those were the only words she wanted to hear.

But he'd never said them. He'd never said anything close. So she had no choice now, Maura decided, but to go.

She would miss Doug's passionate touch. She would never know love like that with any other man. She'd never let anyone that close to her again. The cost was far too great, the loss too painful. Doug was her one love, her true love. She'd never want anyone that way again.

She looked ahead to a solitary life, a life devoted to her child. That Doug wouldn't be there with her was too painful an idea to dwell on, and Maura pushed the thought aside. She felt her eyes well up again with tears and reached for some tissues she'd stuck in her purse on the seat beside her. At the intersection ahead, the traffic light turned from yellow to red and she hit the brake, coasting to a stop.

Suddenly she heard the sound of screeching brakes coming from behind. Headlights flooded her rearview mirror with a blinding glare and the driver desperately pressed on the horn.

"Dear God!" Maura uttered. There was no time for any more reaction. She stared straight ahead, squeezed her eyes shut and folded her arms over her abdomen, instinctively protecting her baby from the impact about to come.

Then she heard the sickening crunch of metal hitting metal and felt her car being propelled forward. She heard herself scream and felt a sharp pain in her midsection as her car slammed into a station wagon crossing the intersection and swerved to a stop. Maura saw the hood of her car crumple like a sheet of paper right before the air bag exploded, filling her field of vision.

Then her head dropped forward and she blacked out.

Maura woke up slowly. She immediately knew she was in the hospital. The familiar sounds and smells had penetrated her subconscious. Feeling groggy and confused, she began to sit up, thinking at first that she was at work and needed to be doing her job, not lying around in a bed.

Then she felt a soft hand on her shoulder. An emergency room nurse, named Mae Li, whom she knew by sight, smiled down at her.

"It's all right, Maura. Please lie back and relax. How are you feeling?"

"I'm not sure," she said honestly. It was hard to talk, her mouth felt dry as cotton. "I have a beastly headache."

"I'll page Dr. Tyler," the nurse replied, mentioning Maura's obstetrician. "She's been waiting to speak with you."

Maura nodded and watched the nurse slip through the green curtains that were closed around her bed.

She knew she'd been in a car accident, but it was all so hazy and muddled in her mind. Then in a rush it came back to her—the glaring lights, the screeching brakes, the sound of metal crunching into metal. Then some flashing images of the police and ambulance drivers arriving at the scene, loading her into the ambulance. The memories were scattered pieces in her mind. She must have lost consciousness a few times. Or else it was just the shock.

She felt a sudden pang of worry. The baby! Was the baby all right? She wanted to ask somebody, but the nurse was gone. She turned and pressed the bedside call button, her hands moving down to cover her lower stomach as she waited. She didn't feel any pain there, she thought, trying to calm herself. Still, the impact could have hurt the baby...

No, it was too awful. She didn't want to think about it.

Tears spilled out of the corners of her eyes and dripped down to the pillow. She felt so empty and alone. Had she lost everything at once—Doug and the baby?

She heard the curtain move aside and expected it to be a nurse answering her call or the emergency room doctor coming to examine her. She couldn't open her eyes for a second, scared to ask the question about her baby.

Then suddenly she felt someone very close to her, holding her, kissing her hair and cheeks. "Maura, thank God you're all right."

She opened her eyes to find Doug leaning over her, his face close to hers, his expression grim. His amber eyes looked so bright as he stared down at her. Yet she still couldn't believe he was moved to tears to find her like this.

When she reached up and gently touched his cheek, he turned her hand to his mouth and kissed her palm. "I'm afraid, Doug...I'm afraid I lost the baby," she admitted on a choking sob. "I'm so sorry..."

He pulled her close, surrounding her with his warmth and strength. "Maura, please, as long you're all right. That's what matters most right now. I saw your doctor for a minute before I came in,'' he added. ''She says it looks good. At least you were aware enough at the accident scene to tell the EMS worker that you're pregnant. You had a sonogram when you came in, but you weren't awake. Your doctor wants to examine you again and give you another test. Then we'll know for sure,'' he admitted with a sigh.

Maura took in his words. She tried not to start crying again but couldn't help it. ''But what if—'' She started to voice her worst fear, but couldn't.

''I know it's hard, Maura. But we'll get through this,'' Doug promised in a comforting whisper as he continued to hold her close. ''We'll try again. My God, when I think of how I could have lost you tonight...''

His words trailed off as he buried his face in her hair and held her even closer. ''I love you so much,'' he murmured in a deep voice.

He pulled back just enough so he could see her face, and he lifted her chin with his fingertips. ''I do love you, Maura,'' he insisted, ''with all my heart and soul. I'm sorry it took me so long to say it. I've just been too scared to tell you. Too scared to love someone so much...and maybe lose you. I think I've loved you for a long time. Since the day I met you. I realize now I just couldn't face it.''

His admission was stunning, and Maura had no words to describe her feelings. He looked down a moment, then back up at her. ''You were leaving me tonight, weren't you?''

''Yes,'' she said, nodding. ''I couldn't stay. I thought you didn't love me. And I couldn't keep living with you that way, thinking you only married me for the baby.''

He gazed at her for a long time, his expression unreadable. Then finally he said, ''Maura…the truth is that when I proposed, the baby was part of the reason. A big part,'' he admitted in a grave tone. ''I wanted to tell you. I really tried, so many times. After that first time we made love, I thought, well, I have to tell her now. But somehow I just couldn't. I guess I already knew how you would react. And even though I could admit to myself how much I loved you, I knew I couldn't stand losing you. So I wasn't honest with you.''

''No, you weren't.'' Though Maura felt a spark of anger at his admission, it was squelched by the joy of hearing that he loved her. She could barely believe it.

''But now you know that isn't true. Can you forgive me?'' he asked quietly.

She met his gaze and quickly nodded, unable to speak.

The look of relief and sheer joy on his face made her heart swell. ''No matter what happens tonight, Maura, I'll always love you. Always and forever,'' he repeated in a heartfelt tone as he pulled her close. ''I'll always want to be with you,'' he promised, his voice full of passion. ''Even if it turns out that we can never have children together. I don't care if we adopt or even remain without a family. All I know now is I couldn't stand being without you. I don't know how I could go on.''

Maura's heart was so full she could hardly speak.

This wonderful, extraordinary man truly loved her. She could barely believe it.

But each time she met his adoring gaze, she knew it was true.

"I love you so much, Doug…I can't begin to say," she whispered. "You must know that by now, don't you?"

"No, I didn't," he admitted, his warm hands caressing her back. "I really thought you still had feelings for Scott. Especially after he called that night and you acted so odd and secretive about the conversation."

She pulled back, shocked to hear how drastically he'd misread her. "No, it wasn't that at all."

But now she could understand why he had become tense and distant around her—while she had thought he'd been having regrets about their marriage.

But instead of saying anything more, she leaned forward and kissed him, relishing the tender pressure of his mouth on hers. Their kiss deepened as Maura opened her mouth under his. She felt the antiseptic atmosphere melt away and felt herself transported to that perfect place where only Doug could take her.

Then the sound of someone clearing her throat made Maura and Doug move apart. Maura looked up and was relieved to see her own doctor. Although Doug had moved away from Maura a bit, he still kept one arm around her shoulder.

"Any news about the baby, Dr. Tyler?" Doug asked.

"The blood tests and sonogram look good," Dr. Tyler replied in an even tone. "You've had some bleeding, Maura, but the baby looks fine. We're going to give you another sonogram now and take a second look. Are you ready?"

Maura looked into Doug's steady gaze and found all the strength and love she needed. She turned to the doctor and nodded. "Yes, we're ready," she said.

Minutes later Maura was wheeled into a small testing room. Doug stood beside her, holding her hand as Dr. Tyler prepared her. The doctor took her time and didn't say a word as she conducted the test. Maura could hardly breathe, she felt so anxious. She looked up at Doug, and he gave her hand a reassuring squeeze. Yet in his expression she could also see distress. Even though he was a doctor, right now he was just an anxious parent.

"There's the baby," Dr. Tyler said suddenly, with a sharp note of excitement.

She pointed to a tiny, blurry image on the screen, and Maura strained her neck to catch a glimpse. She met Doug's gaze and they shared a special thrill that only new parents know.

"He looks beautiful," Doug said in awe.

"Or *she* does," Maura said with an indulgent laugh.

"Sorry, folks, it's too soon to settle that debate. But boy or girl, your baby looks fine. I don't see any problems at all," the doctor said with a finality that was very reassuring.

"You're a lucky woman, Maura," Dr. Tyler added as she removed the imaging equipment from Maura's stomach and pulled off her gloves.

"Yes, I know," Maura had to agree. She felt the tender pressure of Doug's kiss on her forehead and knew now that she was luckier than she'd ever dreamed possible.

"I think you can go now," Dr. Tyler said. "As long as you take it really slow for the next few days. And I wouldn't rush to get back to work, either."

"Absolutely," Doug promised in a stern voice. Maura glanced up at him and saw his most serious expression. She knew she didn't have a chance.

After Dr. Tyler left them, Doug helped her sit up. He put his arms around her and held her close. "The baby's okay," he said simply.

"Yes, thank God," Maura replied quietly.

"But no matter what, we'll always have each other." With his arms still circling her in a strong embrace, he leaned back and met her gaze. "Ready to go home now?"

Maura nodded. "And you don't have to worry," she promised. "I'll do just as the doctor said."

"You better believe it," Doug replied with a short, deep laugh. "Because you're going to have this doctor watching your every move, babe."

His tone was a mixture of protectiveness and passion, and Maura felt a secret thrill. "I would hope so," she replied, her green eyes shimmering with longing for him.

Their lips met in a deep, soul-satisfying kiss, and Maura suddenly realized that this moment, this kiss, marked the true start of their marriage. No matter what the years would bring, she would make a real home with the man she truly loved and would always cherish their life together.

* * * * *

DYNASTIES: THE CONNELLYS continues...

Turn the page for a bonus look at what's in store for you in the next Connellys book—only from Silhouette Desire

AND THE WINNER GETS...MARRIED
by Metsy Hingle
June 2002

One

"**W**here is he?"

Kimberly Lindgren jerked her gaze up from the computer screen as Tara Connelly Paige stormed into the office suite. "Mrs. Paige," she said, quickly coming to her feet to intercept the other woman who, given the high color in her cheeks and the snap in her voice, was furious. "I don't think your brother is expecting you."

"Oh, I'm sure he's not. But he *is* going to see me."

After working as an executive assistant for more than two years at the Connelly Corporation, she had become a master at smoothing ruffled Connelly feathers. Yet something about the fire in this particular Connelly's violet eyes told her this was not going to be one of those times. Still, she had to at least try. "I believe Justin is on the phone at the moment," she said, positioning herself in front of her boss's office door. "If you'll have a seat, I'll go in and let him know that you're here."

"Thanks. But I'll just tell him myself."

Kim didn't move. "That might not be a good idea, Mrs. Paige. Your brother's had a rather difficult morning."

"If that's your way of telling me that Justin's in a rotten mood, I appreciate the warning. Really I do. But it just so happens that I'm in a rather foul mood myself, and Justin is the reason. I *am* going to see him, Kim. Now the only question is whether you're going to move away from that door and let me pass or do I go through you to do it. It's your call, Kim. What's it going to be?"

"Why don't we go in together," she suggested, seeing no alternative. Since Justin really was on the telephone, she tapped on his door and entered without waiting for a response. The sight of Justin at his desk with the magnificent view of the Chicago skyline behind him was something that never failed to make her heart race. But the scowl on his handsome face now made her tense.

"Listen, Marsh, I don't care how busy you are. I want that revised budget and copies of all your correspondence with Schaeffer on my desk by the end of the day. Is that clear?"

Kim nearly winced at the edge in Justin's voice, but it was the way he was rubbing the back of his neck that concerned her. He'd been working too hard again, she thought. Since taking over as vice president of marketing six months ago when his brother Daniel had assumed the throne of Altaria, he'd handled the work of two men.

"I mean it, Marsh. I want everything before the close of business today or you can clear out your desk," he said, and slammed down the phone. Only then did he look up at her. "Kim, I—" He looked past her and, upon spying his sister, his scowl deepened. "I said that I didn't want to be disturbed."

"I know, and I'm sorry for the interruption," Kim began, knowing all too well that Tara couldn't have come at a worse time. "But your sister needed to speak with you, and I thought maybe you could see her for a moment before you leave for your next appointment."

Tara breezed past Kim and placed herself directly in front of Justin's desk. "The truth is that, short of tackling me, Kim did everything possible to keep me out of here."

"And naturally you refused to take no for an answer," Justin replied.

"Naturally. And considering it's a skill I learned from you, big brother, I can assure you that I have no intention of taking no for an answer now."

"I'll leave you two alone," Kim said.

"You might as well stay," Justin replied before she'd taken a step toward the door. "This shouldn't take long, and there are several things you and I need to go over before I leave." He glanced at his watch. "All right, Tara. I've got all of five minutes to spare. So why don't you tell me what's got you so fired up?"

"I'm fired up, brother dear, because you think you've weaseled your way out of being in the bachelor auction fund-raiser this weekend like you promised.''

Justin sighed. ''It's not a question of my weaseling out of anything. I simply can't do it.''

''Why not? And don't hand me that lame excuse that you gave Jennifer about some unexpected business problem that you need to take care of, because I'm not buying it.''

''It's not an excuse. It's the truth,'' Justin countered. ''Whether you believe it or not is up to you.''

''Well, I don't believe it,'' Tara returned. ''Have you forgotten how important this fund-raiser is? That the money raised is going to be used to help the families of slain police officers?''

''No, I haven't forgotten,'' Justin said firmly. ''I've already apologized to Jennifer for pulling out at the last minute like this. But I have an important meeting in New York that afternoon and it would be nearly impossible to get back in time. I'm truly sorry about the fund-raiser, but I promise I'll send a sizable check. There's just no way I can make it,'' Justin said, and there was no mistaking the regret in his voice at having to deny his sister's request. ''I'll admit, I've never been wild about the idea of being in this auction. I only agreed to do it because Jennifer and mother asked me to and I know it's for a good cause. But as much as I hate letting them or you down, there is simply no way I can be in two places at once.''

Kim admitted she hadn't been any keener on the idea of Justin spending a romantic evening with some beautiful socialite than he seemed to be. And she had been relieved when he'd canceled. But now, witnessing Tara's disappointment and Justin's distress at being the cause of it, she couldn't help but feel guilty. Before she could change her mind, Kim blurted out, "Actually there is a way you can do both."

Both sets of Connelly eyes turned to her. "How?" Tara asked.

Kim swallowed. "A couple of things would have to be worked out first, but it is possible."

"What do you need?" Tara countered.

"First you and Jennifer would have to arrange it so that Justin would be the last bachelor to be bid on at the auction."

"That's not a problem," Tara assured her. "What else?"

"Justin's meeting scheduled here Friday morning with the marketing department would have to be postponed until next week."

"That shouldn't be a problem, should it?" Tara asked her brother.

"I guess not." He eyed Kim warily. "What about Schaeffer?"

"Your meeting with him could be moved up a few hours. Say a meeting over lunch instead of one that spilled over into the dinner hour. That way even if your meeting with Mr. Schaeffer spilled over into the afternoon, as long as you made it to the airport by five o'clock or five-thirty, I can get you on a direct flight that would put you back in Chicago in three hours. Allowing thirty minutes travel time to get you from O'Hare airport to the hotel, you could be there for nine o'clock."

"And I can have a driver waiting at the airport to pick you up and take you to the hotel," Tara concluded. She clasped her hands together and smiled. "Please, Justin, say you'll do it."

"Seeing how my assistant has conspired with you, I don't seem to have much choice."

Tara turned to her, beamed. "Bless you, Kimberly Lindgren. I owe you one."

"Not at all. I was glad to help."

"You did a great deal more than help," Tara insisted before turning back to Justin. "Justin, do you realize how lucky you are?"

"I'm beginning to."

Something in Justin's voice and the way he was looking at her caused Kim's pulse to kick. Mortified that he might realize how she felt about him, she averted her gaze. "I'd better go see about making those calls," Kim told them.

"And I've got to go or I'll never make it to that meeting on time," Justin replied, and began shoving papers into his briefcase.

"But we have to discuss your date package," Tara informed him even as he snapped the briefcase shut and reached for his suit jacket. She followed him to the door. "We need to come up with something really special."

"Get with Kim," he told her. "She'll know what to do."

* * * * *

DYNASTIES: THE CONNELLYS

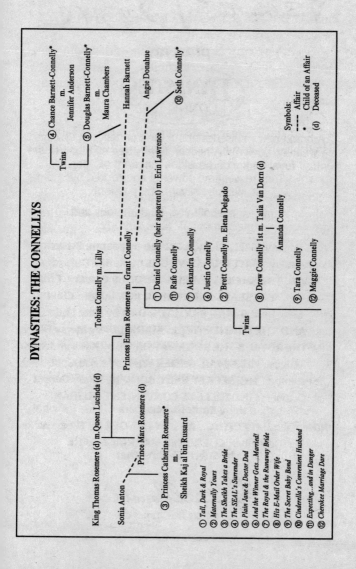

King Thomas Rosemere (d) m. Queen Lucinda (d)

Tobias Connelly m. Lilly

Prince Marc Rosemere (d)

Princess Emma Rosemere m. Grant Connelly

Sonia Anton

③ Princess Catherine Rosemere*
m.
Sheikh Kaj al bin Russard

④ Chance Barnett-Connelly*
m.
Jennifer Anderson

⑤ Douglas Barnett-Connelly*
m.
Maura Chambers

Hannah Barnett

Angie Donahue

⑩ Seth Connelly*

Twins

① Daniel Connelly (heir apparent) m. Erin Lawrence

⑪ Rafe Connelly

⑦ Alexandra Connelly

⑥ Justin Connelly

② Brett Connelly m. Elena Delgado

⑧ Drew Connelly 1st m. Talia Van Dorn (d)

Amanda Connelly

⑨ Tara Connelly

⑫ Maggie Connelly

Twins

① *Tall, Dark & Royal*
② *Maternally Yours*
③ *The Sheikh Takes a Bride*
④ *The SEAL's Surrender*
⑤ *Plain Jane & Doctor Dad*
⑥ *And the Winner Gets...Married!*
⑦ *The Royal & the Runaway Bride*
⑧ *His E-Mail Order Wife*
⑨ *The Secret Baby Bond*
⑩ *Cinderella's Convenient Husband*
⑪ *Expecting...and in Danger*
⑫ *Cherokee Marriage Dare*

Symbols:
- - - - Affair
● Child of an Affair
(d) Deceased

Silhouette *Desire*

presents

DYNASTIES:
THE
CONNELLYS

A brand-new miniseries about the Connellys of Chicago,
a wealthy, powerful American family tied by blood to the
royal family of the island kingdom of Altaria.
They're wealthy, powerful and rocked by
scandal, betrayal…and passion!

Look for a whole year of glamorous and
utterly romantic tales in 2002:

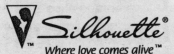

Silhouette®
Where love comes alive™

Visit Silhouette at www.eHarlequin.com   SDDYN02

SINTLTW

ANN MAJOR
CHRISTINE RIMMER
BEVERLY BARTON

cordially invite you to attend the year's most exclusive party at the **LONE STAR COUNTRY CLUB!**

Meet three very different young women who'll discover that wishes *can* come true!

LONE STAR
COUNTRY CLUB:
The Debutantes

**Lone Star Country Club:
Where Texas society reigns
supreme—and appearances
are *everything*.**

Available in May
at your favorite retail outlet,
only from Silhouette.

Silhouette®
Where love comes alive™

Silhouette Books presents a dazzling keepsake collection featuring two full-length novels by international bestselling author

DIANA PALMER

Brides To Be

(On sale May 2002)

THE AUSTRALIAN

Will rugged outback rancher Jonathan Sterling be roped into marriage?

HEART OF ICE

Close proximity sparks a breathtaking attraction between a feisty young woman and a hardheaded bachelor!

You'll be swept off your feet by Diana Palmer's BRIDES TO BE.

Don't miss out on this special two-in-one volume, available soon.

Available only from Silhouette Books at your favorite retail outlet.

Silhouette®
Where love comes alive™

Visit Silhouette at www.eHarlequin.com

PSBTB

You are invited to enter the exclusive, masculine world of the...

TEXAS Cattleman's Club
The Last Bachelor

Silhouette Desire's powerful miniseries features five wealthy Texas bachelors—all members of the state's most prestigious club—who set out to uncover a traitor in their midst... and discover their true loves!

THE MILLIONAIRE'S PREGNANT BRIDE
by Dixie Browning
February 2002 (SD #1420)

HER LONE STAR PROTECTOR
by Peggy Moreland
March 2002 (SD #1426)

TALL, DARK...AND FRAMED?
by Cathleen Galitz
April 2002 (SD #1433)

THE PLAYBOY MEETS HIS MATCH
by Sara Orwig
May 2002 (SD #1438)

THE BACHELOR TAKES A WIFE
by Jackie Merritt
June 2002 (SD #1444)

Available at your favorite retail outlet.

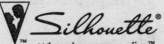

Silhouette®
Where love comes alive™

If you enjoyed what you just read,
then we've got an offer you can't resist!

Take 2 bestselling love stories FREE!

Plus get a FREE surprise gift!

Clip this page and mail it to Silhouette Reader Service™

IN U.S.A.
3010 Walden Ave.
P.O. Box 1867
Buffalo, N.Y. 14240-1867

IN CANADA
P.O. Box 609
Fort Erie, Ontario
L2A 5X3

YES! Please send me 2 free Silhouette Desire® novels and my free surprise gift. After receiving them, if I don't wish to receive anymore, I can return the shipping statement marked cancel. If I don't cancel, I will receive 6 brand-new novels every month, before they're available in stores! In the U.S.A., bill me at the bargain price of $3.34 plus 25¢ shipping and handling per book and applicable sales tax, if any*. In Canada, bill me at the bargain price of $3.74 plus 25¢ shipping and handling per book and applicable taxes**. That's the complete price and a savings of at least 10% off the cover prices—what a great deal! I understand that accepting the 2 free books and gift places me under no obligation ever to buy any books. I can always return a shipment and cancel at any time. Even if I never buy another book from Silhouette, the 2 free books and gift are mine to keep forever.

225 SEN DFNS
326 SEN DFNT

Name	(PLEASE PRINT)	
Address	Apt.#	
City	State/Prov.	Zip/Postal Code

* Terms and prices subject to change without notice. Sales tax applicable in N.Y.
** Canadian residents will be charged applicable provincial taxes and GST.
All orders subject to approval. Offer limited to one per household and not valid to current Silhouette Desire® subscribers.
® are registered trademarks of Harlequin Enterprises Limited.

DES01   ©1998 Harlequin Enterprises Limited

*Silhouette presents an exciting
new continuity series:*

**When a royal family rolls out the red carpet
for love, power and deception, will their
lives change forever?**

The saga begins in April 2002 with:

The Princess Is Pregnant!

by Laurie Paige (SE #1459)

**May: THE PRINCESS AND THE DUKE by Allison Leigh
(SE #1465)**

**June: ROYAL PROTOCOL by Christine Flynn
(SE #1471)**

Be sure to catch all nine Crown and Glory stories: the first three appear in
Silhouette Special Edition, the next three continue in Silhouette Romance
and the saga concludes with three books in Silhouette Desire.

And be sure not to miss more royal stories,
from Silhouette Intimate Moments'

Romancing
the Crown,

running January through December.

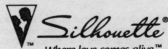